A TEAM TO RECKON WITH . . .

Bert Slaughter

A veteran of two decades with a reputation as the best detective in the Wells Fargo stable. Legendary with a six-shooter, hell with a bottle of whiskey, there hasn't been a hardcase yet who could out-gun, out-drink, or out-ride this incorruptible enemy of injustice.

Ben Slaughter

No one would take him for his father's son—until they cross the sight-line of his deadly Winchester. He has a degree from a fancy college and a way with fancy women—but he's all business when he rides with the man whose blood and name he carries with pride.

. . . SLAUGHTER & SON

SLAUGHTER & SON

E.B. MAJORS

A Warner Communications Company

WARNER BOOKS EDITION

Warner Books, Inc.
666 Fifth Avenue
New York, N.Y. 10103

 A Warner Communications Company

Printed in the United States of America

First Printing: June, 1985

10 9 8 7 6 5 4 3 2 1

One

Over the defenseless and exhausted earth sprawled the heat monster. Sweltering, suffocating all. In the belly of the beast, at its fiery core, lay Alkali Flats; the smoldering hung like a led-weighted curtain over the main street; heat spirals rose from its ruts as if from molten lava. Under the wooden sidewalk stray dogs cringed, their pliant, pink tongues lolling from their mouths, their hot breath issuing forth in labored panting. Dog and man suffered; they waited in vain for rain to rescue them from the heat and their thirst.

Green flies glistened like tiny emeralds under the sun's merciless glare. Enfeebled by it, reluctant to raise their weight into the burning air. The water in the horse troughs warmed to a simmer under the sun's assault. The monster relished its conquest; with every passing hour it grew more intense, more oppressive. It singed and stifled every living thing with its fury. Apart from a few idlers assembled in front of the saloon and the general store in the shadows, not a single resident ventured out of doors, though remaining inside provided no escape from the assailant. Fans abounded, waving furiously and futiley; men, women, and children set sopping wet cloths against their burning flesh in a vain effort to relieve their discomfort.

Three visitors to Alkali Flats stood in the Wells Fargo office in the center of town. With them was Algernon Scoville, local agent for the company, and his assistant. James B. Hume, Chief of Detectives for Wells Fargo, offered the most impressive appearance. He stood six feet one inch tall; he weighed two hundred pounds. His massive shoulders supporting his galluses spread to the width of a small barn door. His hair, previously light brown, had turned white shortly after his sixtieth birthday.

Opposite him, fully two inches taller, but his poor posture settling him to the same height, was Bert Slaughter, senior member of the detective team of Slaughter and Son. Though only forty, Bert had been with Wells Fargo for more than two decades and a detective for the past seven years. While Chief Hume tugged enjoyably on a La Flor de Portuondo, Chicos cigar (thirty-four dollars per thousand), Slaughter masticated with equal deliberation a sizable chaw of Battle Ax plug tabacco (twenty-two cents per pound). One cheek was swollen the size of a hen's egg. He took dead aim at the spittoon squatting by the left front leg of Scoville's roll-top desk. He let fly. The strool streaked toward its target; it missed by a full four inches, puddling the floor. Chief Hume raised his mild blue eyes to the ceiling. Agent Scoville took no notice. He was a pudgy little man somewhat younger than Bert; his roll-encumbered, flabby skin was as pink as the inside of a West Indian conch. He drank unceasingly from a water flask; he perspired copiously. Sweat drenched his hide. Bert appraised him out of the corner of his eye. Agent Scoville, he decided was not a man, but a flesh-and-boiled-shirt-covered machine designed to convert water into sweat. To what purpose, he had no idea, but so abundantly did it flow from him that Bert could almost hear splashing on the floor at his feet.

Scoville's assistant, on the other hand, doggedly refused to sweat. He drank no water; not a single drop emerged from his pores. Bert himself hadn't drunk any kind of liquid since his breakfast Jamoka four hours earlier; he nevertheless sweat. Everyone in the room, everyone in town sweat. With Scoville leading the general outpouring.

But not the glandless, tallow-skinned, undernourished-looking little man chewing his lip nervously and standing beside his superior. Perhaps his skin wasn't skin. Perhaps it was wax. On second thought, maybe he was dead. Upright, eyes open notwithstanding. Bert continued his study of him.

The fifth member of the gathering was Ben Slaughter. He bore surprisingly little resemblance to his father. No craggy, deeply fissured face his, no prominent acquiline nose, no unkempt mustache to cushion it. Only their eyes were similar. Identical. Light blue and gleaming, arrestingly handsome in and of themselves. Ben was shorter than his father, but broader through the chest. Bulkier throughout. Bert's clothes were those of the working ranch hand. Ben preferred a lightweight linen suit. In spite of his father's snide comments, he wore a straw skimmer of the style seen in summer on the streets of eastern cities.

The attention of everyone present was focused on a shiny, new combination safe: 2,100 pounds of steel and fire-resisting materials devised and manufactured by the Vollmer-Bolton Safe and Vault Company of Cincinnati. President Lloyd Tevis of Wells Fargo, had purchased 100 Vollmer-Bolton No. 44 safes for approximately thirty percent of the company's offices on Chief Hume's enthusiastic recommendation. Hume lauded the safe's capabilities fervently and at length over the products of no fewer than seven competing firms. He patted his choice.

"Gentlemen, we have here the finest, most modern safe yet built bar none. Completely fireproof. And burglarproof."

Bert Slaughter grunted. Hume stiffened and fish-eyed him. "Yes?"

"What?"

"You disagree?"

I didn' say nothin'."

"You grunted. I repeat boys, fireproof *and* burglarproof."

Bert shifted his chaw from his left cheek to his right. "Anythin' one man puts together, another can take apart. Anythin'. Law o' Nature."

"To be sure, to be sure," said Hume. His eyes fired slightly. He sucked his cigar and despatched smoke ceilingward. "The point is, how long does it take? Safecrackers don't generaly allot seven or eight hours to the job. Gentlemen, Number forty-four here is far and away the best of a good lot." He ticked off the names of the seven competitors whose safes, in his opinion, had failed to measure up to Vollmer-Bolton's pride.

"They're all good, but this is the best. I draw your attention to the lock. No keys, combination only. Set in the finest, purest high-carbon steel available. In our test, four sticks of dynamite clamped against it and detonated barely dented it. Without the slightest damage to the mechanism. A one-ounce vial of nitroglycerine affixed to the lock failed to inflict even slight damage. Set in a roaring fire for twenty-four hours, not one scrap of paper locked inside was so much as singed. This safe has been dropped from a height of twenty-two feet. The impact shattered an oak plank floor an inch and a half thick. Without any appreciable damage to the body, lock, or contents."

He deposited his cigar in the spittoon. His eyes went to Bert as he did so. Then to the puddle of tobacco juice on the floor. He inhaled sharply and frowned.

"By the Lord Harry it's stifling in here!" He glanced at Scoville's unsweating assistant. "Is June always this hot in this town?"

"Hot?"

Ben grinned, Bert looked bored. Hume went on.

"The legs are permanently fastened to the floor by eight stove bolts. It would be easier to move the building than the safe. Note if you will that the door fits perfectly into its frame. Precison engineering at its finest. It's impossible to drive wedges into the seams to bend the sides outward to allow a crowbar to be inserted between the body and the edge of the door. All six surfaces are fireproof.'' He tapped the door. ''Behind this outer steel body stands a layer of blowpipe- and drill-resisting alloy. Behind that, the inner steel door plate. Next comes the lock assembly, backed by three inches of fire-resistant diatomaceous earth and the inner steel body. With all respect to Doubting Egbert here, I repeat, the Vollmer-Bolton Number forty-four *is* fireproof and burglarproof. It's impregnable. If anyone alive can break into this safe I will personally eat my hat!''

Bert grunted.

• • • •

A week later to the day, a Vollmer-Bolton No. 44 safe was blown open in the Wells Fargo office in Leadville, Colorado, 400 miles north of Alkali Flats; $6,000 was taken. The night after, a second No. 44 was blown in Gunnison and relieved of nearly $24,000. As oppressive as the heat had been in Alkali Flats the week before, it was mild compared to that of James B. Hume's ire when informed that a third safe had been broken into in Durango, southwest of Gunnison.

He, too, exploded. The Slaughters, meanwhile, lingered in northern New Mexico awaiting a new assignment. Word arrived describing the three calamities. Over the Rockies and across the San Juan River they rushed to Durango.

The agent who greeted them appeared utterly crushed by his misfortune. He looked to Bert to be ten years too old for his job, aches and pains and fretting, a confirmed complainer and handwringer. He wrung his hands and shook his gleaming hairless head. He decried his ''rotten luck'' and described what he had found when the explosion rocked him awake and sent him running out into the night.

''It . . . it smelled o' cordite somethin' fierce in here. They was still so much smoke you could hardly s-s-s-see. The d-d-d-door was lyin' on the floor jus' like you see it. Blowed clean off'n the hinges. Not a mark on the safe itself, as you can s-s-s-see.''

Ben knelt. Both the inner and outer plates encasing the

lock were badly mangled. Where the lock had been was a gaping hole. The chief's vaunted diatomaceous earth fireproofing was scattered about.

"I d-d-d-didn' touch a blessed thing. Foun' it j-j-j-jus' like you see. C-c-c-cleaned out for fair. They got near thirty th-th-th-thousan'."

Bert whistled softly. "Anybody see anythin'?"

"Everybody heard. 'Splosion was like to blow every roof off every b-b-b-buildin' in town. They sc-sc-sc-scooped an' ran. Nobody saw nothin', far as I know."

Again he wrung his hands, shook his head, and voiced a heart-rendering sigh.

"Wh-wh-wh-what gets me is the day after it got here, I get a l-l-l-letter from James B. Hume himself. Toutin' to b-b-b-beat the band how burglarproof, f-f-f-fireproof, everythin'-proof it's s-s-s-supposed to be. Hell, it opened up easier'n a tin o' nine-cent sar-sar-sar-sardines!"

"I don't get it," said Ben rising. "If the door's drillproof, as the chief claims, how'd they get the explosive inside? It's obviously been blown from inside. You can see, the combination lock was blown outward. And *it's* not even damaged. Look, you can still turn it."

"Whatever they used, they coulda' circled the lock, lit up, an' blammo." He eyed the agent. "Where was the lock when you got here?"

"Ri-ri-ri-right where you s-s-s-see it. With the door between. Hole an' all, like you s-s-s-see . . ."

"This bunch could be on to somethin' bran'-new," said Bert. "More powerful than dynamite or even nitro."

"Let's get out of here."

"Where to?"

Ben asked for a map. The agent spread it over his desk. Ben found Leadville. He moved his finger down to Gunnison, then down to Durango.

"South southwest, right? In almost a straight line. Which suggests their next move will be Aztec or possibly Floravista, just over the border into New Mexico."

"Ain'-ain'-ain'-ain' no office in Floravista."

"You really figger them for that stupid?" asked Bert.

"To follow a clear-cut pattern? They'd be beggin' to be chased."

"They've followed a pattern up to now, haven't they?"

"That don' mean beans on a platter. They could head in any direction from here. Hume's give 'em a hunnerd o' these safes in a hunnerd towns. They got their pick."

"Is it worth a ride down to Aztec or not? You decide."

"Why me? It's your idea."

"Aztec it is."

A boy about seven, clad in and overwhelmed by his big brother's bibs, appeared in the doorway. So many freckles splattered his face, it looked as if mud had been thrown at him through a sieve.

"Harley . . ."

"*Mr.* S-S-S-Stiers, Hugo."

"Bud Sundstrom sent me to tell you he was lookin' out his upstairs winder last night when them owlhoots blowed your safe. He seed 'em ridin' out. Was 'leven or twelve. Leader was a tall pole. Stringy, coal-black hair down to his shoulders like an Injun. Ridin' a dun-colored stallion with four white hocks an' a white cross on its forehead. In the moonlight Bud could see clear as day, fella only had one eye. The leader, long hair . . ."

Bert froze. The agent responded. The boy embroidered his description of what Bud Sundstrom had seen. Their words reached but failed to enter Bert's ears.

"Which way did they head?" asked Ben.

"Border," said Hugo.

"Aztec."

"S-S-S-South southwest."

Still Bert paid no attention. He turned from the others. He closed his eyes and sent his mind whirling back in time.

Two

Close to 1100 rugged, dusty miles separated Kansas City from Stockton, California. Ariel had gone off to Kansas City to visit her mother. Grandmother Finlay was dying. Ariel planned to stay at least a month. She had debated whether or not to take Ben out of school and with her but decided against it at the last minute. Bert persuaded her that he would be able to take care of him. Off she went on the eastbound stage. In time a telegram arrived with the unhappy but not unanticipated news that Grandmother Finlay had gone to her reward. Ariel would be staying to help with the funeral arrangements. She planned to leave for Stockton on the twenty-sixth. She would arrive home on the twelfth. Just in time to celebrate Ben's birthday, his seventh.

The happy day arrived at last. The stage was due in at four in the afternoon. Ben scrawled ''Welcome Home, Mom!'' on the biggest piece of cardboard he could find.

He nailed it to a broomstick. Together, father and son walked the nine blocks to the Wells Fargo depot. They left Ben's birthday cake, baked and decorated by Mrs. Rowley—their next-door neighbor and Ariel's good friend—the livingroom decorated with streamers and balloons, and the birthday boy's gifts, wrapped by his mother the day before she left, piled on the sofa in the parlor. On the way to the depot, Bert told Ben not to expect the stage to be on time. He warned that the distance, the unpredictable weather, the sorry condition of many roads and bridges, and other factors could delay it at least an hour. Possibly longer.

Bert's heart warmed as he sat on the bench watching Ben study the minute hand as it crawled around the face of the drop octagon clock above the agent's desk. The depot office was gloomy and cramped. Cluttered with furniture and file cabinets overflowing with bulging folders. The depot was next door to a livery stable. When the wind was wrong, it sent its acrid, fetid odors over to visit. Ben took no notice. He was too engrossed with the clock and the minute hand's progress. It had assumed absolute control of this, his birthday.

He sat stock still urging it forward. When both hands finally clicked four o'clock into place, his narrow shoulders slumped in relief. But a quick look out the window assured him that the stage had not yet arrived. He scooted outside with his sign. He took a long, hopeful look up the street toward the east end of town. He came shuffling back in. His sign dragged; his head hung dejectedly. The agent, his assistant, and Bert exchanged winks and grins. Other people came in to wait for friends and relatives.

At twenty past the hour a stage did arrive. The east-bound from San Francisco, jouncing in on its thorough-braces. Its black leather front and rear boots glistened from the thundershower it had just passed through. Its wheels were crusted with mud. The body was spattered up to the leather-curtained windows. Passengers got off, others got on. Their luggage was placed inside the metal fence of the roof.

Ben's patience ebbed as his anxiety mounted. At four-thirty he set his sign down. He planted his chin in his palms and riveted his eyes to the clock. Not a whisper of complaint did he murmur, but he sighed, frowned, and fidgeted, and every so often flashed a questioning look at his father alongside him.

Five o'clock chimed. Bert began wondering and worrying himself. At five-twenty the telegraph receiver clicked. The assistant agent seated himself at the apparatus. He rattled the key briefly. He waited.

Waited.

Five minutes more dragged by. The key came to life clacking loudly. Bert studied the assistant's slender, sensitive face. It darkened by degrees as the message came in over the wire.

"What is it?"

Up came the man's hand silencing him. The agent had joined him at the key. He leaned over and listened intently. His lips moved, mutely forming words.

"Good God. . . ."

Bert jumped to his feet. He grabbed him by the shoulders. The agent shook him off.

"Take it easy. It's. . . . There's been a holdup. This side of Cedar City, Utah. They got the driver, the shotgun, and a passenger."

"Sssssssh!" The man at the key glared. He wrote on a small pad. The apparatus clacked its last. He ripped off the sheet. Bert snatched it from him.

"Pop . . ."

"A woman passenger . . ."

"Take it easy, Bert," said the agent. "It doesn't say which. Three women boarded in Kansas City. They could have picked up even more . . ."

"They coulda' 'all got off before Cedar City except her!" Bert winced. Ben was clinging to his every word. The agent's eyes strayed to the boy. Ben's eyes were round with fear. The color drained from his cheeks. Bert crumpled the paper.

"Let's go back to the house, son."

"NO!"

The shrillness of the one word jerked the agent's head back like a chicken's on the strut. Ben set his small jaw. He grabbed the bench so hard his knuckles turned white.

"On your feet . . ."

"Please, Pop. What's there to go home for? We'll only have to come back."

The others' expressions agreed. Bert ignored them. Still, Ben *was* right, what was there to go home for? An empty house, the living room gaily decorated, the cake, the presents. And no Ariel.

He brightened. "I know what. We got us a little time to kill, what say we walk down to Hager's an' get us a couple ice-cream sodas? With whipped cream an' a cherry sittin' on top. How's that sound?"

"No thanks, I'm not hungry."

"You don' have to be 'hungry' for ice cream. Come on, Ben, this is your birthday. It's time we started celebratin', right?"

"Not without mom."

"We'll jus' start. When she gets here she'll join in. Come on, Ben."

He surrendered. "I guess. If you really want . . ."

Bert ushered him out the door, his hand gentle at his back. Outside, Ben turned to him.

"Did mom get shot? Is she dead?"

"Course not! Why do you say such a dumb thing?"

"The man on the key . . ."

"He doesn' know beans on a platter. It was one o' the two older ladies. For sure. Let's go, I can taste that creamy chocolate already."

They sat side by side at the counter. Ben watched fascinated as the old woman built and decorated sodas in tall glasses. The ball-top faucet gurgled as she pushed it forward, constricting and pressuring the flow of carbonated water. The sodas inflated. She topped them with whipped cream and a shiny red cherry crown.

"Sip slow now," said Bert. "Make it last."

They were Hager's only customers at the moment. The place was immaculate: freshly painted white with a black and white checkerboard floor. Tables lined the wall behind them with spiral back chairs. Bert wasn't particularly fond of chocolate sodas. He didn't much like any flavor. His sweet tooth suffered from neglect; a jigger of rye whiskey would have been far more welcome at the moment, he reflected. But he kept a smile of enjoyment on his face.

He sipped slowly. Three women passengers, one shot and killed. But not Ariel. Not his love. That could never happen. Never. Impossible. Bushwhackers almost never killed passengers; it was something of an unwritten law, even among the lawless. Unless folks were foolish enough to try something. Not Ariel. She never would. Most sensible woman alive.

Alive.

At twenty-five she was still his little girl. At that, she looked no different than on her wedding day, when she was seventeen. Still as slender and pretty. Beautiful. Glistening chestnut hair, dark, flashing eyes, and smile that set his heart aglow at sight. Such a little slip she was, almost frail looking. When they were courting, he'd been afraid to hold her in his arms lest he break a bone. He remembered telling her; how she had laughed. Little girl mine. He sipped and lowered the level to halfway, catching up with Ben.

Lord in heaven but he missed her! Her six weeks away seemed like a year behind bars to him. In solitary. In eight years of marriage they had never been apart longer than overnight. Oh, once in a blue moon two nights, when he was driving the Stockton to Medford, Oregon run. He disliked being away from her even an hour. She hated it. She always looked so relieved when he walked in the door. As if she'd been worried sick he'd caught one on the run. It happened, but not Stockton to Medford and return. There wasn't a more boring route on the whole Pacific coast. A man could drive it asleep on his box.

No. It couldn't be Ariel who'd been killed.

He glanced at Ben. He slurped noisily as he struck bottom. He twirled his cherry stem between thumb and forefinger. Bert smiled inwardly. He seemed not nearly as anxious as before.

He glanced past him down the marble counter to the round, glass-top candy case. He got up from his stool and lay money on the counter.

"You suppose they got any Iceland Mass Squares?"

"OH BOY!"

"Sssssh. It's still your birthday. All day. Birthday's a day you're supposed to splurge. It's tradition. Wouldn' wanta go 'gainst tradition, would you? Hey, we might even find us some peppermint New York Rubber Gum."

"WOW!"

He bought a ten-cent bagful of Iceland Mass Squares and a pack of spearmint gum. There was no peppermint. They stood outside under the awning nibbling the mint-flavored squares. The clock in the window of Bentham's Jewelry across the street read one minute past six.

"Mr. Slaughter!"

It was the assistant agent, still in vest and shirt sleeves. His grin spread his face. He waved and ran up.

"Word just came in over the wire. The lady killed was an older woman . . ."

Bert gasped. He grabbed and hugged him. And danced him in a circle. A man and woman passing ogled them. Bert let him go. He whooped loudly, grabbed Ben, and lifted him high.

"You hear that? She's okay! She's aces! Didn' I tell you? Didn' I? When does the stage get in?"

"Any time now, according to Sonora. Better late than never, right?"

"Aaaaamen!" Bert clapped him on the back. "I sure 'preciate your comin' to tell us . . .

"Boss's orders. Yes sir, she'll be rolling in in five or ten minutes. No more than that." He chortled. "Not unless the bridge over the Stanislaus River's out." Ben gaped. The man ruffled his hair playfully. "Bet your birthday it's not!"

They trooped back to the depot babbling excitedly. The second Bert walked in, his grin of relief vanished. An invisible fist gripped his heart. On the agent's face was a hangdog expression. The saddest face Bert had ever seen.

"Told these two the good news . . ." The assistant stopped and stared.

The agent lowered his eyes sheepishly.

Bert stiffened. "What's the matter?'

"Oh, Jesus . . ."

"Say it! SAY IT!"

"Word just came in from Sonora. They first said it was one of the older ones. They did. We both heard it . . ."

"Yeah, yeah . . ."

"Somebody made a mistake. Not us, Sonora. It turns out it was the younger woman. I'm sorry . . ."

• • • •

They rode side by side at a steady, easy pace through the rugged San Juan Mountains. They crossed the border between the La Plata and the Animas. And veered left in the direction of Aztec.

No sooner were they out the door of the Durango office than Bert crawled into his shell. He was now preoccupied with resurrecting black memories; he refused to talk beyond mumbling single-syllable answers to Ben's questions. He doggedly, with a fierce stubbornness, avoided any mention of their quarry. His reticence failed to faze Ben. He resolved to work on the shell until he cracked it.

"So it's Cutler. So what?" Bert flung him a glare calculated to shrivel him, but said nothing. "There's no reason to go off half-cocked."

"I didn' think we were. We got us an assignment. Culprits to chase. We're on their trail. Isn' that the way it gen'rally works?"

"Surprise, surprise, it talks."

"Shut up."

"Seriously, Pop."

"Don' call me Pop! How many times I got to tell you? My name is Bert."

"Egbert."

"Bert, damnit! Call me it. Or father . . ."

"Father? Are you a priest? Where's your hard collar?"

"You're 'bout as funny as a busted back on the weddin' night. Anybody ever tell you you got a sense o' humor? Don' hol' your breath, nobody's gonna."

"Why so testy? I should think you'd be celebrating. You've been scratching about the territories for fifteen years, and suddenly, smack into our laps he falls."

"We still got to catch the mangy scum."

"We will. All I'm saying is let's deal with it like any other case. Intelligently. Patiently. Let's not get overzealous and careless just because it's Cutler."

"If you mean don' shoot him on sight, you can go fly a anvil. I get that son of bitch in my groove, I'll blow his one good eye through the back o' his head. Watch me!"

"We'll talk about it."

"You talk. An' excuse me if I don' listen."

• • • •

The surviving passengers had seen Rance Cutler close up. His was not a face easily forgotten. The Stockton agent had come to the Slaughters' home a week after the shooting with a detailed description. It was ten at night. Ben was in bed at the time, sleeping as well as could be expected. Bert was unable to sleep at all. Ariel's body had been brought in with those of the shotgun and driver. Her funeral was held two days later. Father and son had stood over her coffin, both staring down at it, dying by inches, their cups filled to overflowing with bitterness. Bert's certainly was. He recalled fighting back the urge to shout. Curse the Fates.

Bitterness filled him. It coursed through his veins, displacing his blood. It rose in quantity in his throat. It settled in a black pool under his breakfast each morning. It simmered all day, heating to a rolling boil by nightfall. It took him to bed with it; it kept him awake to all hours. It shackled him.

Her absence, the emptiness in the house, the loss of her

laughter, the deprivation of her warmth and love ripped the heart from him. He felt hollow. It gave his bitterness even more room to fill. He became so obsessed with hatred for Cutler, so overwhelmed with his craving for revenge, it was not until the day after the funeral that he realized that he was now a widower with a seven-year-old to bring up. With no relatives on either side of the family to help.

When he was on the road driving for the company, he left Ben in the care of Mrs. Rowley. She insisted on it. The Rowleys had a boy a year older than Ben, and two girls younger. When he was between runs and able to stay home, Bert did the cooking and cleaning. He was determined to keep the little house as spotless as Ariel had. In tribute to her memory as much as for his and Ben's comfort. He even tried sewing when Ben lost a button or wore a hole in or ripped his pants or shirt. In time he got so he could stitch a reasonably straight line. But he never did get the hang of threading a needle. Not until he devised his own method. He would rub the pointed end of a second needle with soap, lay the thread carefully against it with the end flush with the point, and poke needle and thread through the eye of the other needle.

Life was not all black. His sorrow, if not his bitterness, eased in time. Father and son, always close, drew closer. They fished, took long walks together, rode out into the valley on the gloriously bright summer afternoons after work. They played catch by the hour. They swam, hunted, picked berries, argued, and talked. How they talked! Six hours at a clip. Well into the nights without even realizing how late it had gotten. So close did they grow in mind, heart, and spirit Bert came to think of them as one person in two bodies.

Two weeks after Ariel's funeral, William Fargo summoned Bert to his office to talk. He repeated his sympathies voiced at the funeral. With Ben in mind, he offered Bert a permanent job as an agent in the first vacancy that opened up. Bert was grateful but unenthusiastic. The work would be unexciting and arduous; but the hours—7:30 to 6:00—would permit him to come home to Ben every night. They would no longer need to depend on Mrs. Rowley.

Four weeks later the main office notified him that the agent in the Rawlings, Wyoming office was retiring. Bert sold the house. They moved to Rawlings.

With him, Bert brought along his carefully and well-reserved bitterness. He vowed to his maker that one day he would catch up with the snake who had murdered Ariel. And blow his head off. He lay in bed nights devising dozens of ways of avenging her death, each more complicated and more painful than the one before. To call him out, outdraw, and outshoot him was the last resort. What satisfaction would there be in that? He wanted to "taste" his death. Bite off a hunk, chew it, savor its succulent juices. When it was thoroughly chewed, send it slowly down his throat into his maw. Where it would sit undigested for days, warming and pleasing him.

Sweet oh sweet revenge!

The Stockton agent who had come to the house described the circumstances of Ariel's murder. The passengers had been ordered out of the stage and lined up at the side of the road to be relieved of their valuables. Cutler ordered everyone to turn out his pockets. Ariel had reached into her bag. He was sitting his horse not fifteen feet from her. He shot twice. Both bullets struck her in the chest. She died instantly.

He blew the smoke from his gun and explained to the shocked onlookers. She was reaching for a Derringer, he told them. He had one of his men turn her bag upside down, emptying it. There was no Derringer. She was mortally afraid of guns. Bert couldn't even get her to hold one.

Life in Rawlings proved as dull as Bert imagined it would be, until Ben turned a corner in his life just after his seventeenth birthday. Bert was home alone one evening. He sat in his easy chair chewing and reading the paper. A knock sounded. It was two of Ben's teachers.

They talked with Bert for an hour. They told him that

his son was a brilliant student. That he far outstripped his classmates in every subject. Bert knew he was smart, but their unstinting praise, their enthusiasm over his potential surprised him. They asked if Ben was planning to enter college in the fall. Bert admitted that he hadn't thought about it. Nor, to his knowledge, had Ben himself. Neither had ever mentioned the possibility to the other.

The teachers trotted out all the reasons why Ben *had* to go to college. For him not to would be unthinkable. A criminal waste of his fine mind. The world was the oyster of every young person blessed with intelligence of his caliber. With his grades he could get into any school in the country, even Yale or Harvard.

In September he enrolled in the University of Virginia. Four years later he graduated *summa cum laude* with a Bachelor of Science degree. At commencement there wasn't a prouder parent in the audience. Tears of joy dimmed Bert's eyes. His chest swelled with pride; he tingled and glowed all over. When the president took him aside at the reception and told him that Ben was in line for a teaching job at the university, it was all Bert could do to keep from shouting hallelujah.

Then the hammer fell. Or rather Ben dropped it.

• • • •

"Did I ever tell you what a jackass I think you were to get into this line o' work?"

"So many times I've lost count."

"In one ear an' out the other. That's sure 'nough a jackass for you . . ."

"This jackass likes the job."

"It's stupid. You're wastin' your life. It's disgustin'! You're 'bout the only man in the entire company—I'm talkin' four hunnerd an' thirty-six offices—an' hunnerds, thousans o' men, who's got a college education."

"That's amazing. I'll try not to let it go to my head."

"A man's got to be king o' all jackasses to stick with a

job that pays as little as this, that's as dirty, dangerous and disappreciated . . ."

"Un. Unappreciated."

A roly-poly badger waddled across the road in front of them. Bert's mount's left forehoof barely missed its tail. It vanished into a thicket. Bert jerked the reins. It snapped the grulla's attention back to the job at hand: getting the two of them up to and over the crest ahead. The mingled scents of red fir, Engelmann's spruce, and yellow pine sweetened the air.

"You're fritterin' away your brain matter like so much sand poured outta' a boot. Workin' at a job that takes 'bout as much savvy as a flea needs to find its way to a dog's ear. Col' blooded murder o' golden opportunity, that's what it is.

"A smart brain is the rarest o' the rare. To be blessed with one, an' to waste it, to as good as reach into your ear, pull it out an' stuff it 'hind a sofa cushion is a sin 'gainst Nature."

"I'd never do that. I might forget where I was sitting. I've told you before, I like the work. It's really that simple."

It was an argument they often got into. It started out in a straight line. Bert gave, Ben took. Then it curved until it came around full circle. It was slippery. No solution seemed able to stick to it. Which didn't discourage Bert from dredging it up.

In his heart he knew why Ben resisted moving on into something more demanding. He was sticking with him out of loyalty. Nothing else. Ben didn't like the work, didn't dislike it. All he was interested in was keeping the team together. It made Bert feel guilty and resentful toward him. And raised his hackles when Ben shied away from discussing it.

Rance Cutler. He had spent fifteen years turning over rocks looking for the snake. For the first thirteen he had neither seen nor heard of him. For most of that time he had lived with the nagging worry that Cutler had gotten himself killed or died. Either would deprive him of his rightful vengeance.

Two years before, their paths had crossed in a little town in west Texas, Gomers Corners or Clusterville. Whichever it was, Bert had forgotten it in the shuffle of events that fell into order that night. Ben was still in college at the time.

Blurred images stained the screen of Bert's mind: they sharpened, clarified. Became vivid. The saloon was a rat hole: dirt floor, bare plank walls, no mirror over the bar. The bar itself was a single board laid across two barrels. Two brands of booze: corn and a rye, take it or don't. A rat hole that reeked of body sweat, stale liquor, and the unmistakeable stench of the sloppily mopped up contents of recently aired paunches. Drunks reeled about cursing; raucous laughter laced the smoke-fouled air. A game of high-stakes stud at a corner table was bringing out the worst in the players: complaining, arguing, threatening.

Bert entered, took one look, and resolved to order, drink up, and get out before the various stinks seeped into his clothing. Before some drunk got his ear and his back up. He stood at the plank bar downing his tumbler of rotgut when who on God's earth should walk in but Cutler. Alone.

Sight of him, immediate recognition—thanks to the Stockton agent's description—sent an audible gasp up and out of Bert's throat. He gaped. Cutler caught his stare and returned it with his one working eye. A regular recognized him and called him by name. It removed all doubt as to his identity.

Ariel's murderer.

Bert's mind and common sense took wing, taking his judgment with them. A spasm of fury so powerful, triggered with such suddenness it started him trembling, took over. He dug his nails deep into his palms, struggling to control himself. He could feel his cheeks warm. The bulge in the vein in his brow. It was all he could do to keep from lunging at him. He wanted to seize and strangle him!

Cutler's lone eye studied him. His curiosity aroused by the all-too-obvious change in Bert's expression at the sight of him. Bert unconsciously sent his right hand to his Peacemaker; he set the heel of it against the grip. A smile came to Cutler's thin-lipped mouth.

Bert took his hand away; he cleared his throat. He was about to confront him when the stud game exploded in loud accusations and a flurry of fists. Over went the table. Chairs slammed to the dirt floor. Guns fired wildly. A stray slug whistled past Bert's ear. He had turned to face Cutler in the doorway. At the first shot Cutler turned and fled. Bert started after him; by now the place was bedlam. A big-bellied man wearing a large, crooked nose took a punch in it. He dropped into Bert's path to the door. In his haste to get out, Bert tripped over him. By the time he regained his feet, he found himself in the center of the brawl. Somebody slugged him in the shoulder, another in the ribs. He fought back out of instinct. Then his thinking switched back on and he realized his mistake. He broke away and got to the door. But thirty precious seconds had slipped past. Outside there was no sign of Cutler.

He went wild. He cursed, whipped his hat off, dashed it to the ground. When he finally cooled down, he wondered what Cutler must have thought, seeing himself stared at so, with eyes blazing with hatred. Still, there was no possible way he could link him with Ariel. He didn't need to, he need only see that the man gawking recognized him. And from his expression wanted him dead. The threat couldn't have been clearer; Cutler's face, ugly, empty eye socket and all, had displayed perfect understanding.

The second time their paths crossed was in the spring of the following year, just before Ben graduated. In Annona, below the Oklahoma line. Cutler and his tribe-of-the-moment had hit the local bank. Bert had joined in chasing them. They'd caught up with and surrounded the lot, only to lose them when a Comanche war party happened by and started potting every white-eyes in sight, making no distinction between good and bad.

Bert got away on a dead brave's pony. How Culter had escaped he couldn't imagine. But he had worried for months after that he had not. And was still worrying right up to Durango, the office, Hugo What's-his-name and Bud Something's description.

Father and son arrived in Aztec late in the afternoon. They split up and moseyed about the little town. Neither spotted anybody that looked like Cutler. Ben rejoined his father in the Aztec House Bar and Beef Grill. A much too distinguished name for a shabby shebang offering little more than bad whiskey, bad company, and eardrum-shattering noise. The bartender, a chesty man wearing a filthy apron and a mustache sorely in need of trimming, proved helpful.

"Ja, they come in." He lowered his massive head to shield his words with his hand. "No mistaking the vun-eyed vun mit the stringy hair. Mean looking . . ."

"How long ago?" asked Ben.

"Hour, hour und a half."

"How many with him."

"Big bunch. You two boys lawmen? Is he vanted? I'll bet he is, in half the stades und all the territories. Who'd he kill?"

"We'd just like a word with him," said Bert.

The man's grin snapped into place so fast it threatened to tear the corners of his mouth. "I bet! You *are* the law, aren't you? Vot, Pingertons?"

"Sssssh. How'dja guess? We'd 'preciate it if you didn' mention to anybody we been askin' after him."

"I von't. I von't. Meeeean face. I've seen bedder looking buzzards." A rag that looked capable of crawling the length of the mahogany under its own power materialized in his hand. He wiped. "Vot'll you haff, boys?"

"Got any Haggerty's Morning Dew?" The bartender stared blankly. "Gimme bar whiskey."

Ben ordered a beer.

Again the bartender leaned over and lowered his voice. "Dey could be coming back."

Bert narrowed his eyes. "They say they might?"

"I got the veeling they plan to hang around avhile. Vun mentioned getting a good night's schleep vor a change. Sounds like either here in town or glose by, vouldn't you say?"

Bert's grunt was noncommital. He drank, grimaced, and drank again. They left, separating a second time to comb the town again. It was nearing nine. Bert checked his Winchester and his gear and fished in his saddlebag for his can of quinine powder. He set it on the hitch rack and plunged his Green River knife through the top. Two elderly women, stern-looking, discouragingly homely look-alikes, schoolmarms, he decided, glided by. They settled their eyes on him as he carefully lifted the knife straight up and licked the quinine sticking to each side of the blade. They started in astonishment. As if he had just opened his wrist and was drinking. His face warmed with embarrassment. He touched his hat brim with his finger.

"Ladies . . . It's for my ague. It's this mountain air. Whenever I come outta' the heat into it, it chills me somethin' fierce. This here quinine . . ."

His voice trailed off. They were surprised but not interested in explanation. They hurried their step. And leaned their heads together to whisper, one, then the other, glancing back at him.

"Keeps away the ague. Aw, what you care . . ."

Hooves hammered the street behind him. A host of riders were coming in. He shoved the can back into his bag. He cinched the strap and ran for the nearest alley, heart up and hoping. He stood in the shadows and watched them pass.

Cutler was riding lead. Bert peered around the corner of the building; his soul sang with joy. He watched them pull up in front of the Aztec House, dismount, and troop inside. They jabbered loudly, pushing one another playfully. Just a bunch of hard-working good old boys taking a night on the town. He waited until the batwing doors swung outward after the last man and then went to look for Ben.

This was it! Cutler wouldn't get away this time. There'd be no brawl, no Indian intruders, nobody, nothing to mess things up. At long long last he was his!

He drew his Peacemaker. He lay it across the flat of his hand and bussed it affectionately.

His!

Three

The outlaws' hideout sat high in the mountains east of Aztec on level ground, surrounded by a sparse gathering of scraggly pines. The house looked very old; it appeared solidly constructed, though. "Probably built by prospectors searching the area for silver," said Bert. Searching the wrong end of the territory.

He and Ben lay prone on a flat rock, hats off, six-guns in hand. They peered over the edge of the rock down at the house. Cutler and his men had dallied in Aztec until around midnight. Then left as they had arrived, in a body. Father and son followed. There were eleven. Ben did not like the steep tilt of the odds. But his concern sparked no reaction from his father.

Ben studied his expression as he rode along beside him. It suggested that of a religious fanatic, busy working himself into an emotional frenzy in preparation for battle against the despised infidel. It troubled Ben. Time had not weakened his own determination to make Cutler pay for his brutality, but he tried his best to keep the thing in perspective. No so his father. Not since Durango. His obsession was clearly taking over.

Overzealousness in a cause is no asset to the aggressor. So mused Ben worriedly. It was a detriment. It obscured judgment, distorted perspective, abandoned common sense. It embraced impulsiveness and rashness. It invited disaster.

He had tried many times to persuade his father of this. All he ever got for his trouble were a nod and a grunt. The grunt was Bert's favorite nonanswer. It commited him neither one way nor the other. They had never been able to discuss dealing with Cutler unemotionally. Twenty seconds into the conversation, the signs always showed: the reddening of his face, the measured syllables escaping from between his tightly clenched teeth, the deliberate avoiding of eye contact.

Ben had long ago decided that *he* would have to be the one to finish Cutler. His father couldn't be trusted with the job. He'd only botch it. He'd go overboard, he'd drown.

Ben had killed seven men in this, his first year with Wells Fargo, all in self-defense. In Bert's quarter century with the company—he had started as a shotgun messenger at fifteen, lying three years onto his age to get the job—he had killed so many he had lost count long ago. He never discussed killing, other than when he talked about Ariel's. And Cutler's in payment for it.

"This is lunacy," said Ben. "Eleven against two. At least eleven. There could be three or four more in there who didn't come into town."

"Scared?"

"You're not?"

"Not a bit. I never let myself think 'bout odds. I wouldn' be alive today if I did."

"Brilliant. That may well be the dumbest thing you've ever said."

"DON'T YOU TALK TO YOUR FATHER LIKE THAT!"

"Ssssh, keep it down. All I'm saying is, sailing in

brandishing the fiery sword of vengeance could get us our heads blown off. So easily. We should bring in the nearest law. Blanco's only a couple miles from here."

"Forget it!"

"No outsiders meddling in your triumph, is that it? No intruders in your hour of glory. You'd rather chance getting us both killed."

"There's no rope 'round you. You can leave."

"Will you listen to reason just once?"

"I'm sick to death o' listenin' to your so-called reason! I know what I got to do. An' you or nobody else is gonna mouth me outta' it."

"Stubborn son of a bitch!"

Bert glared. "I didn' hear that."

"I'll say it again."

"Just shut up. Go ahead, get outta' here. Go back to town an' get yourself where to sleep."

"Of course. I'd be apt to desert you."

"You wouldn' be desertin' nothin'. I'm orderin' you, get the hell outta' here!"

Ben said nothing. He didn't budge. Bert eyed him. He sniffed, then returned his attention to the house. The outlaws had started a fire. Smoke lifted languidly form the chimney.

"If you're stayin', you're helpin'. I don' need a damn audience."

"Stubborn . . ."

Bert slapped him. Hard. "One more peep an' I'll bust you one, see if I don'. Get up an' get 'round back."

"What for? What do you plan to do, circle them?"

"Get up on the roof. Take along your saddle blanket. Cover the chimney. Smoke 'em out. They'll come pilin' out the door, I'll . . ."

"Which door, front or back?"

"Anybody comin' out back you'll be in position to take."

"Not if somebody comin' out front spots me. Look at that roof, it's almost perfectly flat."

"Stop jawin' an' get your blanket."

"Bert . . ."

"All right, I'll go."

"I'll go. DAMNIT!"

"Then move!"

Saddle blanket over his shoulder, Ben slipped around the left rear corner of the house.

"Keep it quiet, for Chrissakes. They hear you overhead they'll plug you through the roof."

He waited; he held his breath and watched. A shadowy figure appeared crouching, inching slowly across the roof to the chimney. Ben straightened. He waved and swept the blanket open like a bullfighter spreading his cape. He was about to cover the chimney when he stopped suddenly. He stood motionless, blanket in hand, neck bent, head thrust forward over the chimney. The smoke rose around him.

"Cover the damn thing!"

Ben draped the blanket shawl-like around his neck. He started back across the roof the way he came. Minutes later, he came running out of breath.

"What in hell . . ."

"Sssssh. Listen. I could hear them down below. As clear as a bell. Get this, they're going to bypass Aztec. They're going to hit Fruitland instead."

"That's crazy . . ."

"I heard them! They're staying her tonight. Tomorrow, probably as soon as it turns dark, they're heading for Fruitland. There's a Wells Fargo office there."

"Who knows if they got a Vollmer-Whatchamacallit safe . . ."

"What difference what kind? We'll beat them there. We can hole up in the office out of sight. Wait for them to show up and take them!"

"You mean ride away now an' leave 'em here? That's stupid!"

"It's not. Why get into a shootout? With a little luck we'll take them without a shot. Set a trap they'll walk right into."

"You hope."

"I heard what they said. You think I'm lying?"

"Course I don't. But *they* could be. Could be jus' mouthin' off."

"Why? How could they know anybody was listening?"

"They could . . ."

"Will you stop it? It's beautiful. We'll catch them with the goods. All the evidence we'll need to nail them. What a break! Thank you, Lady Luck, you are a beauuuuutiful lady . . ."

Bert grunted. The more he thought about it, the more sense it seemed to make. If they did catch them in the act, it would stand up in court. Not enough to hang them, maybe, but they'd at least be put away. All except one. Cutler would never get to prison. Never even get to trial. He'd see to that personally.

Yes, leave them now. Hard as it would be. Catch them later. Ben was right; he was tempted to congratulate him, was about to, when a sudden surge of willpower quelled the urge.

Four

Bert's gaze drifted out the rain-stained window of the Fruitland Wells Fargo office. It crossed the street to the millinery shop opposite. A middle-aged woman was emerging; under her arm was a package. Her closed parasol dangled from her wrist; her sleeves and skirts ruffled as they met the passing breeze.

"Great day in the mornin', look at that! Whatta face! Looks like a raw-knuckle heavyweight in wig an' skirts. Look at that nose! Heaven help her mirror! Don' stare, son, you're liable to crack your eyeballs. Ha! Look at that build. Fatter'n a prize sow. She prob'ly needs a barn door to get inside her house. Ha! Whatta you think she weighs, two seventy-five? Three hunnerd? I'll bet she bust more chairs an' stairs than you can shake a stick at. Ha! By God she's 'nough to make a man run home an' burn the bed!"

His two visitors' startling revelation had plunged Agent E. Floyd Gilhuly into a maelstrom of confusion, where the shark of fear menaced. Bert's impromptu recitation seized his attention. Providing temporary relief.

"The lady happens to be my wife."

Bert swallowed. "You're funnin' . . ."

Gilhuly's stony stare eloquently announced that he was not.

"Pretty dress," said Bert.

Gilhuly ignored him. "But how do you know they plan to rob us next?" he asked, pointedly addressing Ben.

Ben explained how he had come to overhear the outlaws' plans. The overweight target of Bert's derision was bearing down on the office. The ostrich plume floating above her hat bobbed with her every heavy step. Gilhuly opened the door.

"Afternoon, dear heart."

"Supper'll be on the table at six-thirty sharp, Floydie. Don't be late, ducky."

"I won't, sweet-ums."

"Fried pork chops and garden peas. Your favorites. Excuse me for interrupting."

He squeezed her hand. Off she trundled. Gilhuly closed the door and faced Bert. And glared.

"Pretty dress. Real pretty."

"You were saying?" Gilhuly asked Ben.

"Pretty as a picture."

"Do you mind! I'm talking to your partner."

"They'll get here sometime tonight," said Ben. "Probably after midnight, though we can't be sure of the time. We'd like to hole up in here. When they show . . ."

"Just the two of you? You said there were eleven. We should get hold of Marshal Bevins and his deputies . . ."

"We'd rather you didn't. We'll surprise them, get the drop on them. They'll be concentrating on the safe. They certainly won't be expecting anybody to be hiding in here."

"You hope," said Bert.

"Jesus, Mary, and Joseph! This is horrible! I've been agent in charge here six years. Me and Alton Kimmerling. Just us two. He's home laid up with a bad back. We haven't had one single holdup, not so much as a broken window . . ."

"Everybody's luck got to run out sometime."

"Two against eleven. If anything goes wrong they'll wipe you out in two shakes of a lamb's tail. Couldn't Bevins and his men surround the place? You know, a backup. Just in case they're needed. Hide behind rain barrels, across the street in the alley, out back . . ."

"NO!" Bert froze him with a scowl. "We do it like he says. Just us. Too many cooks wreck the soup. We can handle 'em. It's almost six, why don' you lock up a little early? Go home, enjoy your chops an' peas, go to bed early, sleep like a baby . . ."

"Is he serious?"

"Mr. Gilhuly," said Ben. "We know it's upsetting. It can't help but be, but at least we know they're coming. And we can prepare."

"We don' know when, Ben."

"Tonight. That's certain. The minute they're inside we'll surprise them. It'll be all over before they get near the safe."

"I don't understand any of this. Chief Hume claims a four-pound cannonball couldn't break that door. I got his letter around here somewhere. He lauded the safe to the skies!"

"Best in the worl'," said Bert. "But even best in the worl' can be busted into."

Ben shook his head. "Not this one, not tonight."

Gilhuly crouched in front of the safe; he began twirling the combination dial. "The money and valuables in here are going into my middle desk-drawer. There's a lock on it."

"No need for that," said Ben.

Bert gestured him to indulge Gilhuly. "If it'll make you feel better, do it."

Gilhuly did it. He locked about $19,000 in cash, securities, and gold certificates in the drawer. He pocketed the key.

"What I should do is trot everything home and bring it

back in the morning." He made a face. "I don't feel good. Worrying always sets my stomach to flip-flopping."

He got out an already opened packet of Doctor Rose's Dyspepsia Powders. He poured a liberal quantity into a glass, added water, and gulped it down. The taste intensified his look of pain.

"I think I will close up early. Go home and lie down before supper."

Bert nodded. "You'd better, you look sick as a dog."

They helped him close and fasten the green shutters over the windows. He handed Ben the front-door key.

"I've got a spare home. The rear door's bolted top and bottom." He indicated. "When you close yourselves in, bolt this door. Musn't make it easy for them to get in. They'll suspect something . . ."

"We'll take care of everything. You go home and try to relax. It'll be all over by the time you come to work in the morning."

Bert nodded. "You'll come outta' this a hero. You'll get your name in the papers."

"I don't want my name in the papers, thank you! I just want all this behind me. I'm not a well man."

"You do look sick as a dog . . ."

"Must you keep saying that?"

Bert assumed a hurt look. "Jus' sympathizin' . . ."

"I'll see you in the morning," said Gilhuly to Ben. "God willing. I'll light a candle tonight and pray everything goes well. Good luck. Jesus, Mary and Joseph, what a life!"

Away he walked, the condemned man heading for the scaffold steps. Bert waved goodbye.

"He does look sick as a dog. He doesn't like me, did you notice?"

"I wonder why?"

"Hey, he shouldn' go blamin' me his missus looks like a bull buffalo . . ."

"Did you have to go into that ridiculous, windy description?"

"How was I to know they're married?"

"You're not exactly Adonis the hunter, you know."

"Be honest, wasn't she the ugliest, fattest woman you've ever seen or not? I'm talkin' both: ugly an' fat. Combination o' the two."

"Why must you continuously, perpetually embarrass me?"

"You're the one embarrasses me! The way you carry on, there's times I wanta shrivel up an' crawl through a crack in the floor. Tellin' him he's lucky to get robbed. They won' be expectin' us. Nothin' can go wrong . . ."

"The man's half out of his mind with worry. I was trying to allay his fears."

"Tryin' to shovel it up 'round his knees. Wait a minute, where you goin'?"

"To get a room and catch a few hours sleep. We could be up all night waiting."

"Betcha they don' even show. Betcha a quarter. I don' know why I let you talk me into leavin' that place. We had 'em practically in our sights, cornered like a wolf in a cave. An' we walk away. Disgustin'. Why I listen to you I'll never know!"

• • • •

Bert had only his suspicions to shore up his natural pessimism that Cutler and the others wouldn't show. He sat on the floor in Floyd Gilhuly's inner office and stared through the open interior door. The safe stood out of his sight to the left. But they had a clear view of the front door. Father and son waited all night. A longer night for Ben than Bert. It wasn't even midnight before he began complaining. He insisted they'd made a terrible mistake. "Blown their chances right out the window." Ben listened without comment, but the longer his father carried on, the more worried he grew.

Had whoever'd been doing the talking below as he stood over the chimney listening *known* he was there? Had it all been a show for his benefit? If it were, he certainly had swallowed the bait. If Bert was right, he'd never hear the end of it. If they failed to show, if instead they hit Aztec or Blanco or Bloomfield, or went back to Colorado or crossed over into Utah . . . He groaned inwardly.

Bert rattled on. He cited every reason he could think of why the outlaws would not show up. What bothered Ben was his inability to argue with him. He could be a hundred percent right.

Still, he couldn't believe they had known he was standing overhead listening; he had been as quiet as a shadow ascending and crossing the roof.

But even if they hadn't heard him, they could have changed their minds. And right now be on their way to any one of a hundred places. Make that ninety-seven, three down, ninety-seven to go.

There was yet another alternative: they could have quit cold. Divided up the proceeds from Leadville, Gunnison, and Durango and gone their separate ways. It din't seem likely, not with ninety-seven more safes begging to be opened. But it wasn't impossible.

If only he and Bert knew more about Cutler. His methods, habits, tendencies. His weak spots, if he had any. He hadn't shown any up to now. The only thing they knew with certainty was that he wouldn't hesitate to shoot a helpless woman. He was an extremely dangerous man.

Bert won his quarter. The sun came up; it glared fiercely, bleaching the heavens over the Rockies. No sign of the gang. E. Floyd Gilhuly, hurriedly dressed, in need of a shave, red-eyed from lack of sleep, and still looking "sick as a dog" showed up shortly after sunup. And promptly came apart at the seams when Ben told him the bad news.

Bert was all for giving up and leaving town. It took Ben three hours to persuade him to stick with it for one more night. He agreed to, although warning as he did that Cutler could be getting further and further away while they sat like two toadstools.

He was still upset over their leaving the cabin. Eleven birds in the hand were to be squeezed, not let go of. Ben did not argue this. Talking him into staying one more night had exhausted him. By the time darkness arrived and they took up their posts in the inner office, he was so tired he was tempted to stretch out on the floor.

Bert helped him stay awake. Not two minutes passed in sequence without his muttering.

Fruitland tucked itself in and went to sleep shortly after midnight. About ten minutes later father and son stiffened. Hooves. Riders approaching. A number of them. Bert bit off a mouthful of Battle Ax and checked his Peacemaker.

"I'm goin' out front, out behin' the stove."

"Stay put."

"No. If it comes to shootin', we'll be able to get 'em into a crossfire."

"We'll hit each other."

"Bull . . ."

He duck-waddled off. He slipped behind the stove, his finger to his lips. Ben almost laughed. He watched his father seat himself on the floor. He drew his knees up under his chin and chewed away. Gun in hand, finger curled around the trigger.

The riders had pulled up outside. They ripped off the hitch rack and put it to work as a battering ram. They caved in the lock first try. In they boiled. Moonlight slanted through the open door, painting the floor. Briefly. The last man in closed it, plunging the place into pitch blackness. Bert slammed his chaw into his cheek and raised his gun.

A voice growled. "Stand where you are, brother, and you won't get hurt, savvy?"

"Please . . ."

The single word froze Bert. He recognized Gilhuly's high-pitched voice.

Damn! Ben too had heard; he held his play. What else could either do? The slightest move on their part and Gilhuly would catch it. Bert's mind whirled. They'd have to stay clear. Let them blow the safe, clean it out, and follow them when they left. Play for a break. Try and work it so Gilhuly wouldn't be caught in the middle, poor soul.

He'd nearly had a stroke on the spot when they'd told him what was coming. Right now his heart must be pounding fit to split!

Somebody struck a match. Bert recognized Culter and Gilhuly. With two guns at his back. Bert eased back out of sight, for fear that one of them might suddenly turn and look behind them. A candle was produced. It was set in its drippings on the floor in front of the safe. One of them knelt in front of it, concealing its light.

Bert watched helplessly as Cutler opened his penknife and poked inside the letter "o" in Vollmer. To Bert's astonishment, he poked a hole the size of his little finger tip in the steel plate. Then, using a piece of wire, he fished about three inches of fuse out of the hole.

"Stand back, everybody."

He struck a match.

"Don't do it, PLEASE! Gilhuly was shaking all over. "There's no money in there, there's nothing. I SWEAR!"

They snickered and laughed in chorus.

"You lie in your teeth." Cutler leered at him.

"It's the truth! As God is my witness . . ."

The fuse sizzled. Bert plugged his ears. The door blew. Smoke billowed. They attacked the safe like coyotes setting upon a buffalo carcass.

"It's empty!"

"I told you . . .," said Gilhuly.

Cutler glared, "You knew we was comin . . ."

"Let's get outta' here, Rance."

"You knew. How?"

"They told . . . I mean every office with a Vollmer-Bolton safe knows. You've been blowing them . . ."

"Where's the money?"

"RANCE!"

"In . . . in . . ."

"WHERE?"

"RANCE!"

"The whole town's wakin' up . . ."

"We gotta git!"

"All right, all right . . .THE MONEY!"

"In the middle desk-drawer."

"Open it. MOVE!"

"Rance, they's lights goin' on 'cross the way. You can see through the door crack . . ."

Gilhuly fumbled with the drawer key. He dropped it. Cutler cursed. He slapped him viciously and kicked the drawer front. The lock shattered. He jerked open the drawer. Overturning it, spilling its contents.

"That's more like it . . ."

They scooped up the money.

"Let's go!"

In ten seconds they were out the door and galloping off. Taking Gilhuly along. Bert stood in the doorway, gun raised, aimed at the back of the last one. Ben came up alongside.

"Don't do it. They'll kill Gilhuly."

"They'll kill him anyway."

Bert spat juice. He holstered his gun and started off. "Of all the stinkin' luck. You stick here . . ."

"What for?"

"STAY! Find out where he lives. Go see his missus. She prob'ly tied an' gagged, if they didn' kill her. They likely did. An' wire Hume, tell him the doors are packed with dynamite."

"At the factory."

"Stay here in town. I'll be back. Maybe an hour, maybe two days . . ."

He started for the corner of the building. His grulla waited in the alley. Ben followed. Bert whirled on him. He grabbed him. He slammed him savagely against the brick wall.

"DO LIKE I SAY!"

Ben watched him ride off. His dust climbed slowly into the moonlight. What a mess, he thought. Poor Gilhuly. Bert didn't stand a chance of rescuing him. Which wouldn't prevent him from trying. He was right: Cutler had no choice but to kill the poor man. He'd watched him poke a hole in the door. Knew the dynamite was inside, with a fuse ready and waiting for a match.

And Bert. One man against the lot. He wouldn't let that slow him down, but his courage didn't alter the odds. He was furious leaving. By the time he caught up with them he'd be in a boiling frenzy. A wild man!

What a mess . . .

Five

AS YOU ADVISED WITHOUT REVEALING REASON FOR INQUIRING HAVE ESTABLISHED OFFICE DOORS ASSEMBLED AND MOUNTED SEPARATELY BY ECCOLS COMPANY KC STOP ACCORDING TO VOLLMER-BOLTON PEOPLE STOP ADVICE STATUS WF AGENT AND WIFE STOP JOIN PARTNER ASAP STOP MAINTAIN CONTACT THIS OFFICE KEEP US ADVISED

JBH

ABDUCTED AGENT STILL MISSING STOP WIFE RESTING COMFORTABLY STOP PARTNER NOW GONE TWO DAYS STOP LEAVING NOW TO FIND STOP ADVISE YOU ASSEMBLE ALL AVAILABLE INFO INCLUDING PIC RANCE CUTLER STOP HOLD FOR OUR FUTURE REFERENCE

BS

James B. Hume's spacious and well-appointed corner office on the top floor of the Wells Fargo & Company's express department building on Sansone Street near Halleck in San Francisco was eminently suited to his position and importance. His new posture-chair behind his enormous flat-topped desk suggested an upholstered throne. Flowers overflowed three large vases. The walls were adorned with framed photographs of Henry Wells, William Fargo, President Ulysses S. Grant, and other dignitaries. The gleaming windows looked out upon the incomparable blue beauty of the bay. Not a single cloud smudged and sun-drenched azure sky.

In spite of his elegant and attractive surroundings, Hume was uncomfortable. He fidgeted in his chair. He perspired. Upset by the presence of President Lloyd Tevis sitting opposite him, he clasped and unclasped his hands nervously. Hume had been loyal friend, confidante, and admirer of both Henry Wells and William Fargo, the company's founding partners. But their successor stirred mixed feeling in his breast. Tevis was a lawyer from Kentucky. He had been unusally successful in business before the lure of gold drew him west some twenty years before. He had arrived in California and applied his fine mind to various ventures. These included a water-supply company, telegraph companies, real estate, and mines. He was successful in every one.

He had invested heavily in the Central Pacific. Daringly. For it was at a time when the line was making its slowest and costliest progress over the Sierra. At that time the directors of Wells Fargo showed little interest in railroads. They did not consider them a serious threat to stagecoaching. But when the Central Pacific broke through the mountains and passed Reno, Nevada, the new, upstart express company directed by Tevis began to compete with Wells Fargo. The prize: the much coveted express business between the Reno railhead and Virginia City, 20 miles to the south. Too late, Wells Fargo's directors awoke to the realization that the future would ride on rails rather than coach wheels.

Their shortsightedness was to cost them dearly. Wells Fargo was forced to pay Tevis $5,000,000 for the single piece of paper that had granted his express company exclusive rights on the railroad. Wells Fargo would survive, but its losses suffered in the rate war with Tevis's company sent its stock plummeting from $100 a share to as low as $13.

Tevis, meanwhile, had been secretly buying it up at the depressed prices. At a meeting with William Fargo and the directors in Omaha, Tevis announced that he now controlled Wells Fargo—lock, stock, and Concords. The directors had no choice but to hand over the company.

It was the triumph of his triumphant career. But his strategy did not endear him to James B. Hume and others loyal to Wells and Fargo. Still, he *was* the boss. And the chief could scarcely fault him on either his energy or his astuteness. He was a doer: he saw nothing as impossible. There seemed no limits to his power or his luck. When Tevis talked everyone listened. Even James B. Hume.

Lloyd Tevis was not overly impressive looking. He could easily be mistaken for a bank clerk. He combed his thinning gray hair across the front of his pate to the right. He affected a somewhat scraggly paintbrush beard. He wore no mustache. He was tolerably good looking, but his only truly striking feature was his dark, deep-set eyes. At the moment they gazed through the smoke rising from the ash of his Old Judge cigarette in its black ivory holder.

"Is this Slaughter capable?"

"Yes, sir. Both are. Particularly the father. In my view, the best man on the force. He's been with the company twenty-five years. He's loyal, tough, shrewd, absolutely fearless. Father and son are our number-one team. their record is most impressive."

If this impressed Tevis he took pains not to show it.

"How did the younger one say they hit on this business of the dynamite being secreted in the door?"

"He didn't go into detail, sir. My guess is he spotted the gang at work through a window."

"I thought they broke in at night . . ."

"Ah. . . ."

"Wouldn't the shutters have been closed? If they weren't they should have been. Never mind."

Tevis drew on his cigarette. He pursed his lips, driving color into them. He sent a white gossamer wave floating toward the window.

"Dynamite planted inside the door. Extraordinary. Straight out of a dime novel. Who was it recommended we select the Vollmer-Bolten Number forty-four?"

Hume felt his cheeks warm. Tevis knew full-well who had done so. It was a game he enjoyed. If it had a name, it would be called "keep the help off balance." He cupped his ear as if Hume had already answered. And he'd missed it.

"I did."

"You did, didn't you? I'd forgotten. Didn't you see a Number forty-four put through some kind of torture test?"

"Yes."

"Fireproof. Burglar proof. Most extraordinary invention since the wheel."

"I hardly expected somebody would load the doors with dynamite."

"Please, who could? Don't misunderstand, I'm not faulting your judgment, Jim . . ."

The hell you're not! I'd like to know what you call it. And don't call me Jim . . .

"Pity we ordered so many, Jim. Half a dozen would have been enough for starters."

"Sir, those old Dumbrille crackerboxes we had spotted about the territories have been on their last legs for years. A six-year-old could break into any one with a hoop stick. I've got a file as thick as your fist from agents complaining about them."

"Mmmmm. I wonder how thick a file you'll get on the Vollmer-Boltons?"

Tevis smiled icily. He got up. Hume relaxed. Tevis sat down, Hume tightened up.

"You think the Slaughters will catch this bunch? I mean before they open up twenty or thirty more?"

It was a stupid question from one reputedly so brilliant. But then it wasn't a question. He was only baiting him. Hume tapped Ben's telegram lying on the desk before him.

"They've identified the leader. He . . ." He stopped abruptly.

"What?"

"Nothing, sir."

"What do you men, 'nothing'? You look like you've been struck from behind. Speak up, man."

"I was just thinking. They took Agent Gilhuly with them. The poor man's chances don't look very good . . ."

He wasn't thinking about Floyd Gilhuly's chances. He was thinking about Rance Cutler. He had read the name in Ben's wire, but it hadn't made any particular impression on him. Now he suddenly recognized it. And recalled Cutler's earlier association with the Slaughters. And just as suddenly it wasn't a case anymore. It was a private feud. Great Swith!

"With your permission, sir, I'd like to wire every office within a hundred mile radius of Fruitland. The Slaughters will be needing all the help they can get. We'll get as many shotgun messengers in there as we can. And the local law . . ."

"I wouldn't waste my time, Jim. The Slaughters are on the move. Nobody's going to be able to catch up with them. What you should do is alert the possible target offices. Tell them what's going on so they can take necessary precautions."

"That's already been done, sir."

"Good boy, Jim."

Tevis left. He left the door ajar behind him. Hume closed it. He raised his eyes imploringly.

"Egbert, wherever you are. Put your private squabble aside. Just wrap this mess up and deliver the culprits. You can do it, pleeeeease . . ."

• • • •

Bert sighed as he sighted the huddled form lying in the ditch ahead. Floyd Gilhuly lay face down. Two bullets in his brisket and a pleading expression fixed in death on his stubbled face. Bert rolled him back over after examining him. He looked about, fixing the location in mind. He had come about five miles straight south down the only road in sight. Cutler and his men would be likewise restricted. They'd awakened the town; they knew they were being tailed. What they didn't know was that a lone man was doing the chasing.

It was rough, isolated country. The Canyon de Olo Amerillo lay ahead. To the right rose Beautiful Mountain. Further on, Ford's Peak shoved its crest into a cobalt sky liberally sown with stars. The peak resembled a crudely hewn stone ax blade.

The wind sang eerily through the stunted pines and rustled the tall, desiccated grass. He gazed pityingly down at Gilhuly. One of his murderers had accorded him the ultimate insult: he'd stolen the poor man's shoes. Missing as well were his watch and billfold.

His poor wife would be shopping for widow's weeds. If she herself had survived the gang's visit.

He remounted the grulla and resumed following. The road appeared little traveled. The moonlight was cooperatively bright, their tracks easy to follow. Two hundred yards beyond where he'd found Gilhuly's body, the trail deserted the road. Their horses' hooves trampled the tall grass to the left, heading up and over a narrow pass. He followed. He reached the top and descended to a fairly level stretch. He heeled the grulla, sending it bolting forward.

Over the next two miles he rode it into a mild sweat in hopes of closing the gap. He came to a large outcropping. He rounded it and pulled up. Ahead about 300 yards and to the right a fire flickered. He dismounted and led the horse forward. After a bit he stopped and hobbled it behind a convenient boulder. The grass here rose to a height of two feet. Several boulders and outcroppings offered good hiding places. He cocked the Winchester, cradling it in his left arm. He crouched and moved forward.

He moved to within a hundred feet of their fire. They sat around it. They were passing a bottle and jabbering loudly. He recognized Cutler, who lay on the ground, his head in his hands, elbows high. He had kicked his boots off. He puffed on a stogie. He looked the picture of relaxation. Bert, lying prone, got Cutler's head in his sights. He gripped the trigger.

He squeezed and stopped. And swore. Why in red hell couldn't he shoot? Why couldn't he kill him? Why shouldn't he? The first reason he thought of was because his friends would swarm over him like a cloud of gnats before he half-emptied the clip. He'd perhaps take a few, but in the end would catch it for sure. And wind up living more than ten seconds longer than Cutler.

How he hated him. There were no words to describe it. Despised the air he breathed! But he couldn't shoot now anymore than he could back at the office. Only now Cutler had no shield, no hostage.

How had he come to bring Gilhuly along? Why? He'd done nothing like that in Leadville, Gunnison, or Durango. What made him change tactics? Did he have some instinct for impending danger? A built-in feel? It was uncanny. It was a kick in the head!

He grunted and lowered his rifle. No sooner had he done so then he heard a soft rustling behind him. He froze.

Snake!

He rose slowly. He was in the midst of turning when a voice growled.

"Hold it . . ."

• • • •

The robbery and Floyd's Gilhuly's kidnapping were Fruitland's crimes as well as Wells Fargo's. Marshal Howland Bevins demanded to be included in the investigation. Ben could see no reason why he shouldn't be. Not until thirty seconds after they met.

"I be the law here in Fruitland, Johnny. This is my show. You're welcome to tag along . . ."

"That's very gracious of you, Marshal."

"Think nothin' of it. I got me three deputies and Clyde Ratchford. He's part time. Not much good, but he's willin'. And he don't drink. We're headin' out the south road in five minutes. You comin'?"

Ben wondered briefly why it had taken Bevins nearly two full days to decide to join the hunt. *He* had an excuse for delaying. Two excuses: Bert's orders. The need to wait for word from Chief Hume.

They rode out. They found Floyd Gilhuly's body in the ditch where Bert had left it. Sight of it visibly paled Bevins' cheeks. He and his men exchanged anxious glances. It occurred to Ben that none of them had ever even seen a corpse before under such circumstances. Bevins glanced his way; worry darkened his face.

"They got to be across the Chaco and into McKinley County by now. Outta' our jurisdiction. Outta' Sheriff Cumberland's, too. I guess that makes the ball game all yours, Johnny." He grinned. "Wish you luck. We'll just take poor Floyd's body back to town. No need for you to dally."

His abrupt change of heart should have annoyed Ben. Instead it came as a relief. He heeled his horse, waved, and sped off. Better no help at all than halfhearted.

Had Bert caught up with them? he wondered. He hoped not. Still, nearly two full days had slipped by. Something must have happened by now. Knowing him, knowing the frame of mind he'd been in when he left, he'd caught up all right. And? He'd have to be out of his mind to invite a showdown. Had he? He wouldn't put it past him. He spurred his horse; he picked up the pace.

Six

Bert faced Cutler. The outlaw's one eye stared. His brow crinkled in puzzlement.

"I know you . . ." Bert averted his eyes. "I remember. Gomers Corners, Texas. The saloon. An' last year, too. You were with that posse that chased us outta' Annona. Hey, how'd you get away from them Comanches?"

"Stole a brave's pony . . ."

"Hey, me too! I played it smart like a fox. With all them dead layin' around I decided I'd play dead. Smack in the middle o' all the shootin' an' noise an' smoke I picked me a arrow up off the ground. I busted the shaft in half an' lay down 'tween two dead braves with the feather end in my fist. Pretendin' it was shot into my chest."

One of his listeners chortled and slapped his thigh. "That was some good trick, Rance."

"Shut up, R.B. Nobody asked you. An' wipe the liquor off'n your chin." Cutler spoke without taking his eye off his captive. "Who are you, anyhow? What's your gripe 'gainst me? Must be a big one. Long, tall, an' grindin' . . . Look at his eyes, boys. Ever see such pure hate? Look at 'em, they're boilin'!"

Bert curled his lip. He said nothing.

"I just asked you a question, fella? That night in Gomers Corners I couldn' take my eye off your face. What's your bitch? TALK, DAMNIT!"

"Murderin' son of a bitch . . ."

"Murdered who? That agent fella back in the ditch? I didn' shoot him."

"I did!" R.B. puffed his chicken chest proudly.

"Tol'ja you had the wrong man."

"Bastard . . ."

"Hey, you stop callin' me dirty names. You got me mixed up with somebody else. For sure . . ."

"Like hell. You killed my wife."

"You're a liar! I never killed a woman in my life. Not a white woman. Tell him , boys. Does Rance Cutler shoot women or children? Never once. Swear on the Bible. Oh, I've crossed with a few good ol' boys in my time." He smirked. "I'll let you guess who won . . ."

"Outside Cedar City, Utah. Fifteen years ago. You held up the stage."

"Never been near Cedar City. Not within a hunnerd mile."

"Lyin' bastard!"

"Look at that hate, will you . . . You'd like to kill me so fierce it's chewin' up your insides. It's turnin' you inside out." He rubbed his chin and stared. "So what am I s'posed to do with you? I can't let you walk, not with that hate. Not even takin away your weapons. You'd sneak back an' smash me dead with a rock."

"We can't take him with us," said the man standing at Bert's elbow. His muzzle was hard against his ribs.

"Who says we can't? Who's givin' the orders 'round here, Arthur Todd? Me or you?"

"You, Rance."

"Then shut your face."

Another man stepped forward. He had been going through Bert's wallet. Cutler snatched it from him.

"What you got?"

"His . . . Guess what? He's a detective with Wells Fargo."

"Are you now?" Again he smirked. "You don' look like no detective. Where's your bowler hat an' broadcloth suit? You really Wells Fargo?" He slapped Bert. "Answer me."

"Murderin' son of a bitch . . ."

"You mean to say you been trackin' us all by your lonesome? Was you in Fruitland? You musta' been, else you wouldn' be here. Where'd you pick up on us? Durango? Gunnison? You'd best find your tongue, brother, 'fore I smash you proper."

"Why don' you shoot me, get it over with."

"You askin' me to shoot you? Hell, I couldn' do that."

"I will," piped R.B.

"Shut up, R.B. No, I got me a better idee. Arthur, you got the list. Give it here." He knelt by the fire and studied the paper handed him. "Las Palomas."

"It's down below on the Rio Grande," said a voice from the rear of the circle drawn up around Cutler and Bert.

"Our next stop. 'S a good long haul from here, right?"

"Two hundred sixty mile," said another man.

"We'll take this old boy with us. You bein' a Wells Fargo man, you can't help but be a help when we visit the Wells Fargo office down there." He chuckled. "I like this, boys, I purely do. We got us a full-fledged Wells Fargo detective's gonna help us rob the company. Is that rich or is that rich?"

Everybody laughed. Except Bert. His expression didn't change; he said no more. He was too busy thanking God for sparing him, at least until Las Palomas. Two hundred and sixty miles. At least five days away.

He'd get away from them. Get a gun, come back, and kill Cutler once and for all. If he had to kill every other one to get to him. In his mind he turned in his resignation to the company. Temporarily. He had private business to clear up.

Business fifteen years overdue.

• • • •

Cutler was as shrewd and as careful as he was vicious. Bert never got near a chance to escape over the next five days. They rode him untied in the center of the group. But when they stopped, even if only to relieve themselves, they tied his hands behind his back. "To relieve him of temptation," as Cutler put it.

They crossed the dried-up Cuchillo Negro River early the morning of the fifth day. Around ten o'clock they came within sight of Hermosa Creek. It, too, was dry. They camped on the bank. The had come to within about two miles of Las Palomas. Bert wondered. Was this to be their last job? Possibly.

Would they take him with them when they left? Probably not. Cutler wanted his little joke: to rob a Wells Fargo office with a Wells Fargo detective along. When the joke was over Cutler'd have no further need for him. He was making friendly overtures to him. Bert refused to return them in kind. He could see Cutler was laughing at him behind his amiable mask.

He pumped him about the holdup outside of Cedar City fifteen years before. Bert had told him once that he'd shot Ariel; as if he didn't know! He saw no reason to repeat it. Or go into detail about it. Cutler saw it differently. Bert fleetingly wondered if his conscience might be troubling him. Impossible. How could anything bother something which somebody didn't have?

He wasn't all that pleased with his own conscience. It could prove an unwelcome burden if and when the chance came once again to blow Cutler away. A chance that looked discouragingly distant at the moment. He sat on the bank with them, his wrists secured behind his back.

"It's gettin' hotter an' hotter," said Cutler. He eyed the

glaring sky, shielding his eyes from the sun. "Gimme some water, R.B.

"Fresh out, Rance."

Everyone was, except Arthur Todd. He was also, shortly, when Cutler handed him back his empty canteen. Arthur tipped it end-up and frowned.

"Cheer up, Arthur Todd, we'll be goin' into town soon. We'll get you a lemon squash an' us a little somethin' to light the ol' fire."

"You think we oughta show ourselves in town? In daylight?"

"Didn' I jus' say we're goin' in?" He clapped a hand on Bert's shoulder; Bert shook it off. "We want all the good folks to get a look at my friend, Mr. Wells Fargo. Excuse me, *Eg*bert."

"Jus' Bert."

"But they's a egg in front o' it on the card in your billfold. Wanta see? Want to, *Eg*bert? That's a funny name. Egbert. Isn' that a funny name, boys? His mama musta' been 'spectin' a egg when he was borned. Some dis'pointment you turned out. Har har . . ."

"Scum."

"Jus' as scum as you're gonna be after you help us turn over the office. Scum o' the earth. Wanted for robbery, murder. Donald . . ."

"Yeah?"

"Get out that harmonicky o' yours. Let's have us a little tune. How's about *The Engineer's Daughter*."

Donald began to play. Badly. Sourly. Bert lay on his side ignoring their raucous singing. He soon fell asleep.

• • • •

Las Palomas was about the size of Fruitland. It was built around two crossed streets instead of on either side of a single main street. Wells Fargo was housed in an adobe brick building on a corner. It displayed the customary iron shutters painted green at the windows. The freight depot stood next door. The loading platform jutted out onto the sidewalk. Cutler, Bert, and the others stood in twos and threes across the street in the shade. The town seemed to be prolonging its afternoon siesta. Few pedestrians were abroad. The only wheeled traffic to be seen was a fully loaded manure wagon. It passed trailing its powerful and ungodly stench.

Cutler wrinkled his nose. "Whatta dump. How can folks live in such a nothin' little hole? Did you see that saloon?" He elbowed Bert. "Makes that hole in the wall in Gomers Corners look like the Palace Hotel in Kansas City."

"You been to Kansas City?"

"Sure." He laughed and winked at the man on his other side. "We had us a little business with some boys in the protective door business there, right Donald?"

"Little business. Lotta' profit." Donald tittered.

"You betcha."

The setting sun slowly stretched the shadows eastward. Darkness would arrive in less than three hours. Then the wait would begin for the town to go to sleep for the night. Was this to be the last nightfall he would ever see? wondered Bert. Forty years of sundowns. A hatful. *Was* the hat full?

Arthur Todd called out as he approached them. His high-pitched voice ripped into Bert's thoughts. A raw kid, he mused, measuring him. No six weeks off the farm. Likely wearing the first boots he'd ever owned. No more than three of his men approached Cutler in years. Most were still in their teens. Learning their trade from the master. Fun, excitement, profit, and an early grave.

"We gonna kidnap this agent like we done the one back in Fruitland?" Arthur asked.

Culter shook his head.

"Why not?" asked R.B. He was even younger looking than Arthur Todd. He came up behind him, spurs jangling. His wide, deceptively innocent-looking blue eyes questioned.

"We snatch him, we got to end up killin' him, that's why not . . ."

"Hostage is good pertection."

"Gilhuly slowed us down."

"Tolt us where the money was hid."

"You asked a question, I answered." Cutler fixed him with a steely stare. "You got a itchy trigger finger, scratch it." R.B.'s eyes shifted to Bert. He leered. "Not him, little britches. He's all mine."

R.B. shrugged and walked back to where he'd come from. Arthur Todd followed, leaving Bert and Donald and Cutler.

"How long you givin' me?" asked Bert. "I mean if you're gonna do it, why don'tcha get it over with?"

"Listen to this, Donald. What's the matter, you on pins an' needles? Give us a break, Egbert, don' push. Don' be no spoilsport. Don' start bellyachin', crawlin' . . ."

"Nobody's crawlin'."

"Think o' it thisaway, you're a volunteer. You come to us, we didn' go out lookin' for you. Be patient, you'll die soon 'nough. And you known why . . . One of us got to, and it sure as hell ain' gonna' be this ol' boy." He clapped his hands together and rubbed them briskly. "Whatta you say we all go get us somethin' to chew on? We got a job to do, man can't work on a empty stomach."

• • • •

Cutler had dispatched two men to check the layout of the office and the depot earlier. He sifted their information and decided to break into the depot at the back, and break through the inside door into the office. Neither door offered much resistance. They crowded around the candle, set in its drippings on the floor in front of the safe.

"Pay 'tention, Egbert," said Cutler. "You're 'bout to see somethin' that'll shock you out from under your hair."

"You're gonna poke a hole through the 'o' in Vollmer an' fish out the fuse, right?"

Cutler scowled and swapped questioning looks with Donald. The wire was produced, the hole poked in the "o". The man doing the poking gasped.

"Damn!"

"Whatsa matter?" asked Cutler.

"No fuse . . ."

"They's got to be. Gimme that thing. Move aside. J.B., hold that candle so's I can see . . ." J.B. did so. But more light failed to produce a fuse. "GODDAMNIT! BASTARDS SCREWED UP!"

"Whatsa matter?" asked Arthur Todd.

"Whatsa matter, whatsa matter! You blind? They forgot to tape the fuse in place 'fore they puttied up the hole an' painted the name on."

"Maybe the fuse got loose, slipped down. It's there, it's got to be. Lemme try . . ."

"Shut up an' get away!"

Bert smiled to himself. First time in a long time, he reflected. Cutler's friends had not slipped up. Ben had informed James B. Hume and Hume had sent word to all the office with No. 44s. The doors had been dismantled, the explosives and fuses removed. So that ended that brief crime spree. Though what good that was to him was unclear at the moment.

"Let's get outta' here," said a voice behind him.

"Shut up!" said Cutler.

"He's right, Rance, give it up. We been here too long already."

"All right, all right." He flung the wire from him. "Go out the same way we come in. No talkin', quiet as can be. MOVE!"

They headed south out of town. Bert was lodged in the center of the pack as usual. Surprised, amazed he was still alive. He couldn't understand why. Not with the mood Cutler was in. He was livid. He fumed and seethed and cursed and snapped like a wolf at a bone whenever anybody spoke. In time everyone shut up, leaving him to his muttering.

No one followed them. No explosion to rock the little town awake. Above, the North Star hung on a straight line to the right of the bowl of the Big Dipper. Midnight. They rode a good ten miles by Bert's estimate before Cutler raised his arm and ordered a stop.

He tied Bert's wrists.

"You could tie me in front, you know, so's I could sleep on my back."

"I could. An' you could bit the knot loose. I'll tie you frontways. Only I'll have to gag you."

"Forget it."

The flickering campfire reddened Cutler's lean face. It set his long, greasy hair gleaming. His eye drilled his captive. Bert knew what he was thinking: when, where, and how. He asked for a chaw of Battle Ax. Cutler fed it to him. Then answered the question in Bert's mind.

"We're headin' for Mexico."

"It figgers."

"That's been the plan since Leadville."

"That's why you been workin' your way south."

"That's why. You figgered that, eh?"

"An egg-brained idjit could figger it."

"How'd you figger out the dynamite was *inside* the doors all the time?"

"Li'l bird told me."

"Get some sleep."

"What for? I won' be needin' any. We both know I'll never see the border."

"There you go again! Tryin' to pin me down. You're startin' to get on my nerves, you know that? Funny Knowin' you're gonna get it is gettin' on your nerves. You badgerin' me 'bout it is gettin' on mine. Tit for tat, eh? That's rich . . ."

He sobered. He leaned down, bringing his ugly eye socket to within two inches of Bert's face. "You really wanna know when? I mean '*zactly*? I'll tell you . . ."

Bert held his breath. The breeze snatched at the dying fire. Ripping the flame, passing on.

"On secon' thought, better you ask your little bird. Sweet dreams, Egbert."

Bert lay on his side awake, listening to the chorus of snoring around him. The air had cooled considerably, but the sand against his cheek was still warm. He was positioned so he could see Cutler sleeping. His head was in his hat; he breathed heavily, his nostrils fluttering.

Bert stared at him. Hating his every breath. His secure grasp on life. His power over his own. Cutler smiled; his eyelid parted.

"Tomorrow, Egbert. Bright an' early. An' in a way you'll never guess if you try from now to then. Good night."

• • • •

The situation harrowed Ben to the quick. At every turn in the road he expected to come upon Bert's body in a ditch. As he and Bevins had found Gilhuly's. He could be certain of one thing. By now Bert had caught up with Cutler, and even if Cutler failed to recognize him, had given himself away. Cards on the table faces up. Straightforward, direct. No cat and mouse play. Hopefully, the one thing his father wouldn't reveal was that he, Ben was trailing them. In spite of his frustration, he couldn't be so rash as to betray him.

Should Cutler get the upper hand, Bert's chances would be nil. Less than zero. It would be obvious to him. He wouldn't be taking foolish risks.

But for some reason he had a sneaking suspicion that Cutler already had him skewered. And turning slowly over the coals. Not that he didn't have great faith in Bert. But good luck didn't come easy to him.

"Hand in there. Hang tough, I'm coming . . ."

He planned to make up time by riding late into the night. And getting back on the road before sunup. The first two nights he averaged less than four hours sleep. By noon of the third day he was groggy. The heat was no help. Nor the strain of anxiety. He rode a four-year-old bay mare with just enough devil in her to give her spirit. But she was tiring. He could feel it. The moment was coming when she would pull up and refuse to go a step further. Regardless of how soothingly he cajoled. She'd have to have a full eight hours that night.

They crossed the Plains of San Augustine. They followed the Alamosa twisting southward, keeping the long ridge of the Black Range running north to south on the right. Just after nightfall he decided to give it up. He fed and watered the mare. He ate half a can of cold beans. He huddled under his blanket and went to sleep.

The only thing he could be sure of was that he was on the right track. Their continuing southward movement down through Colorado and into New Mexico suggested they were on their way to Mexico. A problem. Big problem. A man could lose himself so easily in the Sierra Madre Occidental. The American authorities rarely crossed the border. The Mexicans couldn't be bothered chasing. And so the mountains were overrun with *Yanqui bandidos*.

He slept.

He ran out of the sun into the store. Into a world that shattered the eye. And assaulted the nose with a variety of odors, so many it was impossible to distinguish any one from the mass. The potbellied stove squatted in its sandbox in the center of the floor. Its stovepipe ran straight up to the ceiling. There it bent, crossed over to the top shelf stacked with washtubs, and pushed through the wall.

Two ole men played checkers on a board set on a barrel at the far end of the counter. A woman stood looking over her shopping list. Mr. Schofield patiently awaited her pleasure.

Ben saw them all. Ignored them all. He pulled his hand loose form Bert's and ran to the back and the Wonderful Corner. That's what it was. So-called by young and old. Into the heart of the cloud of delightful aromas he ran. Immersing himself in it. Inhaling deeply. Sucking his lungs full of its indescribable sweetness. Other odors that were not candy filled the store. But none, not even those of tobacco and coal oil, strong as they were, reached into the Wonderful Corner. So powerful was the commingling of odors already there.

The sweets: mouthwatering molasses taffy. Succulent sugar plums and stripped peppermint sticks. Sparkling, sugarcoated gumdrops in a dozen different colors. Ju-

jubes. Marshmallows. Licorice whips in their glass jars. Pungent wine-balls, "all-day" suckers that never made it beyond the ten-minute mark, so scrumptious were they. Peppermints, hoarhound squares, fancy lemon drops, strawberry, pineapple, Yum Yum Squares, Liberty Bells, Iceland Mass Squares, Fancy Cocoa Tablets, Jaw Breakers, Daisy Squares, twist stick candy and mince pie cuts and on and on and on.

How could one choose? Impossible. And when you did you were disappointed. Having selected this instead of that, too much licorice, as delectable as it was, not enough chocolate. Or vice versa.

And when you got to the bottom of the bag. Down to the last gumdrop or final jujube and all you had left was the faint odor of the contents wafting upward from the emptiness you closed your eyes. And saw again the Wonderful Corner. And you, beginning the all-important, most sacred solemn process of scrupulously careful selection.

It was the only way to buy candy, dad always assured him. He knew, he knew everything. Best of all he let *him* do his own choosing. While he wandered about the store looking at merchandise. Looking with no real intention of buying, other than perhaps a plug of tobacco. Or his favorite Brilliantine Hair Oil. Or maybe a can of quinine powder. If he felt the ague coming on.

He would be given the bag to hold and Mr. or Mrs. Schofield would select his choices. Allowing for his sudden changes of mind and lengthly delays while he pondered. It was soooooo hard to choose. There was a limit to how much he could spend, usually ten cents. Dad would let him go over a whole penny if he just couldn't make up his mind between a licorice whip and spearmint drops or whatever choice happened to come last.

It always took ten or twelve minutes to fill the bag. And in spite of dad's warning to take his time, when they got outside all his willpower deserted him. "Slow down" only temporarily slowed his chewing. Never his hand. But then six-year-olds can't be expected to exercise self-control in such things. Dad's grin, the way he shook his head and clucked, told him that was so.

The Wonderful Corner. And the wonderful circus parade of glorious tastes that marched into his mouth. To be welcomed by his appreciative tongue. And moved about inside, touching every taste bud. Chewed or sucked or chewed and sucked and sent sliding down his throat to his grateful stomach. An experience like no other. An adventure without equal.

A shame it only came once a month. When it was over it seemed like years before time for the next visit to paradise. But it always did. And always proved just as difficult in the selecting. Just as delightful, delicious. But always followed with the same misgivings over choices. And the disappointment that it was all over much too soon.

They would sit together on the bench in front of the Caster Brothers' Buggy Shop while he ate. Never once did Dad ask for a taste. He offered, though somewhat half-heartedly. Dad always declined. And bit off a chaw of his Battle Ax. He often wondered if he did so to quiet his sweet tooth. Or because he really felt like a chaw.

They would sit in the warm sun. Eating and chewing. Both talking with their mouths full, which Mom would have cautioned them was "not nice."

Together. Father and son. Man and boy. Bert and Ben. Like the nation itself, one and indivisible.

• • • •

High on a thermal draft a buzzard sat. Pushing in a slow circle, its blacksnake neck tightly tucked. Its wings spread nearly four and a half feet to their fingerlike top feathers. Soaring, staring downward from 6,000 feet at the group of inert figures surrounding the dead fire.

By Bert's reckoning they had camped about ninety miles north of the border. He was the first to awaken. The sun had yet to completely clear the horizon. As white as a shroud it stared back at him. Filling with fire, preparing to pour it over the land. To cook man and beast in their skins.

To punish the world of southwestern New Mexico. For what reason Bert had never been able to fathom.

Perhaps it resented the presence of all things that grew. Mobile and stationary alike. Considered them intruders and was bent on burning them out. Who could say what the sun thought? He had a hard enough time trying to figure what was in mere mortal Cutler's mind.

He looked over at him. He pulled at his bonds. Cutler had tied him just right. Not tight enough to hurt enough to keep him from sleeping; not loose enough to permit any play. He was smiling in his sleep. Bert guessed that he was dreaming about the upcoming execution; his subconscious already savoring the satisfaction.

"There's no damn justice in this worl' for sure . . ."

He looked north. Back the way they had come. Prompting the sudden wild hope the he would see Ben astride his mare approaching.

What he did see chilled him. Cutler had bedded them down in an area filled with lava tables. And guarded by magnificent volcanic buttes standing like monuments to gods. Conencting one butte to the next were unbroken lines of Indians. They sat their ponies stock still. Their eyes fixed on the campsite. Butte and lines formed a horseshoe around them a mile distant. At least 400 savages. The only break in the line was to the south where the way narrowed and squeezed between lofty cliffs. Offering the perfect ambush.

Defying the sun, the breeze came to life. It whipped feathers and buckskin trousers, but not one man moved a hair. They sat, they stared.

"Cutler . . ."

Cutler mumbled in his sleep. He shifted his body. His licked his lips and opened his eye slowly. Warily.

"Visitors."

He saw and swore. "Whatta they want, do ya think?"

"Your hair. Your guns an' your belly for their knife."

"They're not movin'."

"You noticed."

"What are they?"

"Indians."

He snapped up to a sitting position. He rubbed his eye and spat. "Jesus . . ."

"This neck o' the woods they could be Mimbres. Maybe Chiricahuas. Some kinda' ragheads. The good ol' bandy-legged butchers o' Mangas Colorados."

"He's dead."

"His spirit lives on. Take a look."

The Apaches' appearance, and in such large numbers, stirred mixed feelings in Bert. It could delay his own coming execution. Or just change his executioner. If he had to die, it was comforting to know he wouldn't be alone. On the other hand, death from any source wasn't a welcome prospect. And would hurt.

Still, maybe this was the break he needed. . . .

"Whatta ya gonna do? You sure don' have 'nough coffee to go 'roun'." Bert leered at him. "This'll be interestin'. They're holdin' all the picture cards."

"Shut up, I'm thinkin' . . ."

"You do that. Meantime, here they come."

Cutler stiffened. He could not tear his gaze from the sight. His body slumped with relief when only half a dozen savages broke out of the horseshoe. And started toward them on foot in single file.

It appeared to be their chief with a five-man escort. Each brave carried a nine-foot lance tipped with iron with strips of red cloth with eagle feathers attached tied around the point grip. They also carried bows and arrows. All wore Apache boots pulled up over the knee for protection against cactus. All were painted for war. The chief wore a yellow headband. As they neared, the entire horsehoe edged forward. Tightening ranks.

"No rifles," said Cutler.

One by one the others were waking. A few raised their voices at the sight. Cutler barked them quiet.

"They got rifles alright," said Bert. "Not a lot, maybe, but they always manage to get their hands on some. Squint an' you can see. Rifles don' make any difference. Any one can hit a rabbit or a man easy as pie at a hunnerd,

hunnerd an' fifty yards, bow an' arrow. Whatta beautiful mornin'! Whatta great lookin' day! Makes a man glad he's alive!''

"Whatta ya think they want?''

"Anythin' you got, Includin' you hair an' your life.''

"Apaches don' take scalps. Everybody knows that . . .''

"Remember to tell 'em if they try. Remind 'em.''

"Whatta they want?'' asked R.B.

Cutler cut him short with a look of pure disgust. "Shut up, young'un!''

"They look like a buncha' little kids, Rance,'' said Donald. He giggled.

Bert laughed. "Isn' this somethin', Cutler? To be out here in the middle o' nowhere with this sorry collection Buncha' milkfed greenhorns you laughin'ly call a gang. An' four hunnerd ragheads come callin'. Closin' in. Prayer time, everybody.''

"You're crazy!'' R.B. glared. "There ain' no more'n three hunnerd.''

"R.B., you are boss simple.'' Cutler shook his head. "You an' your dumb-ass mouth'll be the death o' me.''

"He'd best get in line.''

Cutler scowled at him. Bert could see the fear welling in his working eye. Sweat glistened on his forehead and upper lip. Chief Yellow Band had stopped about fifteen feet from them. His escort came up on either side. He towered over his men. Had Mangas Colorados, who'd reputedly stood six foot six, been alive, Bert would have taken this one for Red Sleeves. Such height was rare among the eight tribes. The chief's features were sharply chiseled; his skin was redish copper and unlined. He would have been handsome, but a livid scar started two inches above his left eye and came straight down through it. It guttered his cheek down to a point at a level with the base of his nose. The wound did not appear to affect his eyesight. The eye looked as clear as the other one.

The horseshoe continued to tighten until the mounted braves had drawn to within a hundred yards. Bert glanced about. Cutler's men were reacting in various ways. Most were round-eyed and gulping down their fear. Only R.B. was too stupid to be afraid. He looked defiant; he looked absurd. Bert sighed. All it ever took was one to upset the apple cart. The other two exceptions to the group were Donald and Arthur Todd. They looked more curious than afraid.

"I got me an idee," said Cutler between clenched teeth.

"Oh, mother . . ."

Bright ideas were the last thing they needed at the moment. Before Bert could stop him, Cutler strode brazenly up to the chief. He whipped out his iron and shoved it against his stomach. The escort braves stiffened; they readied their lances.

Bert threw up his hands. "For Chrissakes . . ."

"Shut up. Come up here an' tell the red bastard . . . One false move an' he's dead."

"You tell him. Look at him, he's worried sick."

The chief had raised his hand. He moved it slowly to his right. His braves relaxed. Cutler looked up at his eyes. He looked as relaxed as a sleeping baby. The muzzle still pressed against him he grinned down at the outlaw.

"He don' savvy," said Cutler. "Tell him! TELL HIM!"

"He savvies. He's readin' you like a book. Gettin' a big kick outta' you. This is the mos' fun he's had all day. He know you won' dare shoot."

"Watch me."

"You do an' you'll be dead before he hits the ground. He . . ."

A gun exploded behind Bert. Pain stabbed his ears. He watched appalled. Once of the escort braves grunted; he grabbed his stomach and dropped. The outlaws shouted and sprang into action. In a split second all hell exploded.

Bert bellowed loudly; waved his arms, appealing to all of them to stop. Only Cutler paid any heed. To Bert's surprise, with guns going off all around them, he lowered his gun. But before he could stop his men, they gunned down all four remaining braves.

For some reason nobody dared shoot the chief. Bert couldn't be bothered wondering why. He was suddenly too busy worrying about his own safety. With no place to hide, he stood rooted.

Chief Split-Eye's smile had fled his face. But in spite of the tumult around him he had not moved a hair. He stood as before: arms folded. Black eyes questioning Cutler. His men lying dead at his feet.

At the first shot, the tightening horseshoe of savages charged. Barreling in they came, screams, arrows, and a flurry of slugs preceding them. Bert threw himself flat; he covered his head with his hands. Arrows came singing in; they thwunked into the ground all around him. Other targets were less lucky. Three of Cutler's gang died screaming, cursing, kicking. Two more fell wounded.

The dust raised by the attackers rose in a cloud so thick Bert could not see two feet in front of him. Screaming, whirring and thwunking arrows, snorting, pounding ponies were all around him. He started up. Ready to make a run for it. In any direction. Praying he could make twenty yards using the dust for cover.

A thought skidded through his mind; at that very instant an arrow struck between his feet. He watched it vibrate to rest. He snatched it up, he broke it in half. And lurched forward toward the narrow pass to the south. He had not taken four steps when he tripped over R.B. He lay on his back, his chest filled with arrows bunched an protruding like procupine quills. In his hand was his smoking gun.

It was R.B. who had triggered the action. Stupid jackass! Taking his cue from the equally stupid Cutler. Down on hands and knees after tripping, Bert dropped flat. His legs lay over R.B.'s. He turned over on his back. He gripped the half-shaft feathers up and held it against his heart with both hands. He let his head fall to one side and closed his eyes.

On raged the massacre. Gradually the shooting became sparser. It finally stopped altogether. Out of the continuing din came Cutler's voice, bellowing, "We surrender, we surrender!" Bert still held the arrow in place. He chanced a quick look. The dust was settling; he could see the survivors raising their hands. Again he closed his eyes. And held his breath.

He felt a foot against his ribs.

"*Umaha oota. OOTA!*"

Dust clogged his nostrils and stung his eyes. He opened them. Towering over him was the chief. So much for canny strategy, thought Bert. The chief smiled. He reached down and snatched away the broken arrow and lifted him to his feet as easily as if he were a small child. He patted Bert on the head and smiled again.

The breeze sprang up. It cleared away the last of the dust.

"GODDAMN STINKIN' LUCK! GODDAMN R.B.! GODDAMN DUMB SON OF A B . . ."

The brave standing closest to Cutler slapped him sharply. Bert watched in silence. What a bonehead, he thought; what a collection of boneheads. Bottom of the barrel. Dumped into saddles, armed, and set loose to blow safes. And kill anyone who got in their way. What a damn disgrace to humanity!

Though what difference did it make who or what they were now? Or what they'd done. Put up a fight or submit; either way they were dead. If not here and now, soon enough.

Everyone. Himself included.

Seven

James B. Hume stood at his window looking out at the rain-battered bay. He tugged on his La Flor de Portuondo, Chicos cigar. On his handsome face was a bemused expression. Lloyd Tevis sat in his visitor's chair. Erect. Preoccupied. Engaged in fitting an Old Judge cigarette into his holder. Getting ready to contribute to the cloud of smoke nudging the ceiling. Tevis cleared his throat. Tensing Hume.

"The Leadville office was the first one hit. Isn't that so, Jim? It is. When they examined the wreckage, how is it, I wonder, nobody noticed the hole in the letter 'o' in Vollmer?"

"The door was badly mangled. The combination lock was blown clear. The same thing in Gunnison and Durango, too. All three safes were hardly scratched."

Tevis lit and puffed. "What's being done about the

people in Kansas City who assembled and installed the doors?''

''The police are working on it. I know one thing, the company's main office in Cincinnati is full of red faces.''

''And Wells Fargo's full of red ink.''

A knock. Hume's secretary poked her head in. She held up a telegram.

''Excuse me. This just came in from Las Palo-something in New Mexico.''

''Not another one!'' Tevis threw up his hands.

''Thank you, Miss Preble.'' Hume read hurriedly. ''Hold everything . . .'' His worried look gave way to relief. ''Good news. They didn't get a penny. The agent got word in time and cleaned out the door. Bless his soul!''

''I don't suppose anybody bothered to catch the culprits.''

''He doesn't say . . .''

Hume handed him the wire. Tevis scanned it. ''B.S.?''

''Ben Slaughter. He's evidently still tracking his father. Who's been chasing Cutler and his gang.'' He moved to a wall map. He located Las Palomas. ''The parade's moving south. Cutler's heading for Mexico, apparently. If he gets into these mountains just below the border we'll never catch him. The Mexican Army won't even be able to. Wouldn't bother to try. This is where Geronimo hid from General George Crook and Nelson Miles. He'd still be there if he hadn't come out of his own volition.''

''Get in touch with young Slaughter. Tell him as soon as he catches up with his father, the two of them can drop it. No sense wasting manpower on a wild goose chase. Do you agree?''

''I . . .''

''You don't. All right, we'll talk about it.''

Hume sniffed. *What you mean is you'll talk, I'll listen.*

''What have we got so far?'' Tevis ticked off the essential facts on his fingers. ''Three safes blown and robbed. The fourth a failed attempt. All other Vollmer-Bolton safes discovered to contain explosives defused. Presumably. Certainly should be by now. The ones responsible in Kansas City in the process of being rounded up.

Cutler and his gang out of the picture. Have I overlooked anything? I don't think so."

"We're assuming they're out of the picture."

"I must have misheard you. I thought you said if they get into those mountains . . ."

"We don't know as they have yet."

"They're certainly getting close." Tevis waved the telegram. "They were in Las Palomas yesterday; by now they should be well south of there."

"Who knows where they are? It's possible Bert Slaughter's caught up with them."

"I doubt that. He's operating on his own. One man against a gang. I can't imagine he'll give them much trouble. I hope he's got sense enough not to try anything . . . No, he hasn't caught them; the boy won't. Jim, I say we close the book on this one. File it and forget it. We've got too many brushfires need stamping out, and too few stampers. Like I said, it's silly to waste manpower. Wire the boy, what's his name again?"

"Ben."

"Tell him as soon as he catches up with his dad they're to call it off. As far as the company's concerned, it's all over. Have them report back here or to wherever you need them."

"With all due respect, sir, the company's out a sizable sum. Letting this Cutler and his brood get away with fifty thousand dollars could give other outlaws ideas. Besides, they murdered one of our agents."

"They did, didn't they. Too bad, but those things do happen."

"Sir . . ."

"The actual figure is forty-nine thousand six hundred and sixty. Plus twenty-two thousand eight hundred book value in securities and twenty-four thousand to the penny in gold certificates. Total: ninety-six thousand four hundred."

"As I said, a sizable sum."

"I wouldn't go losing any sleep over it. The Vollmer-Bolton people are liable up to their necks. They reimburse us and they collect from the Eccols Protective Door Company. Eccols' insurance will cover their losses . . ."

"It may not."

"Who cares? What's important is we get ours." He got up to leave. "Get in touch with young Slaughter. Tell him we're calling off the dogs." He snickered and shook his head. "Dynamite and a fuse hidden *inside* the door. Extraordinary. Mark my words, Ned Buntline'll write a dime novel about this one. Give us some free publicity. Oh say, congratulations, Jim, you're doing a bang-up job. Stay on top of things. Good man. Keep me memoed."

Out he strolled, trailing a slender plume of smoke after him, leaving the door ajar.

Eight

Worry, like a fever, can reach a dangerously high level if unchecked. Take control of a man's thinking; weaken his powers of judgment. It can be cruel. Merciless.

It had been six days since Ben had last seen his father. One hundred and fifty anxious, discouraging hours. Broken only by sleep; from which he awoke as tired as when he dropped off. His imagination took no pity on him. He pictured all sorts of terrible things happening to Bert. Each one ended in his dying.

He arrived in Las Palomas late in the afternoon. He went straight to the Wells Fargo office. The agent in charge showed him the candle drippings scraped from the floor in front of the safe. He showed him the hole in the "o" and the wire bent into a hook Cutler had thrown aside.

So the gang had shown up. Had tried and failed to open the safe. And gone away empty-handed. Had Bert been with them? Ben wondered. For the hundredth time. He decided he must have been, and still was, if Cutler hadn't killed him. Over the past 250-odd miles, every corner he'd rounded he expected to find Bert. Lying in a ditch as dead as Floyd Gilhuly. Expecting to made the chase the most nerve-wracking ride he had ever made. By the time he reached Las Palomas, he was so wrung out he barely had the strength to sit his saddle. His horse, too was exhausted. "Beat to fetlocks," Bert would have said.

Not finding him in a ditch was no proof he was still alive. The only thing it did was convince him that Cutler had his father. The likelihood was developing into certainty. Much too fast.

He left Las Palomas just after sunup. Still tired, more discouraged than ever. He tried his hardest to dismiss his worries; he pictured Bert perched on a rock. Chewing. Relaxed. As fit as a Lowendall's Artist fiddle. Jumping to his feet and roaring greeting. But in his heart he knew it was a hope too far-fetched to take seriously.

As if things weren't going badly enough, a half-mile south of town trouble met him. A rattler came slithering up out of the ditch and crossed the road directly in front of him. Down came the bay's hoof squarely on its rattles. It sprang in retaliation, spooking the horse, throwing Ben. Down he came headfirst. Striking hardpan, missing by under four inches a jagged rock that could have split his skull. And dump his brains in the dust. Away slithered the cause of it all. Its victim much too unconscious to notice.

He woke up in a doctor's examining room in Las Palomas. His head had been magically transformed into a church belfry. His bell clanged loudly. Brutally. Sending slender darts of pain shooting outward from the center of his brain. Tinting his immediate surroundings alternately blood red and jet black with each stroke of the clapper.

"Ohhhhhhh myyyyyy Goddddddd . . ."

"Lie still, son. You got a fairly nasty concussion there. You're lucky it's not fractured. What were you trying to do, bust up the Hillsboro road?"

The doctor's high-pitched cackle intensified the clanging.

Ben winced. He uttered a groan and sent his hand slowly upward to his afflicted head. He grit his teeth and gingerly touched the spot. His head was cap-bandaged. The doctor held up a mirror.

"No blood. Just a good shaking up. Picture a chuck-a-luck cage and dice. Your skull, your brain. It could be worse, you could have broken your neck."

The doctor was in his middle years. His small head was crowned with an untrimmed thatch of cornsilk-colored hair. It sprang away in all directions and shrank his little face against his head. His skin was deathly white with pale red blotches. He looked about forty pounds underweight. He appeared to be afflicted with a permanent grin.

"My horse . . ."

"She's okay. Better than you. The fellows who found you stashed her in the livery stable across the street. She's fine. Not a scratch, not a bump. Of course you won't be needing her for a spell anyway . . ."

"How long?"

"A week at least."

"I can't stay that long. I'm following somebody . . ."

"Your following days are over. For awhile. Does it hurt?"

"It feels like the Liberty Bell."

"Ah, so you're the guy who cracked it. How's about some popskull?"

His terminology ill-suited the occasion. But his liquor was welcome. Ben sipped. The warmth chased down his throat and settled around his cold bean breakfast. Happily, it dulled the clanging.

"By the way, my name's Wysock. No jokes, please, I've heard them all. Who are you?"

"Ben Slaughter."

"You say you're following somebody? Errant husband? Wife? Holdup specialist?"

"That's close. I'm with Wells Fargo. I really appreciate your taking care of me . . ."

"I'm a doctor, what do you expect?"

Once more his high-pitched cackle broke the rhythm of the clanging bell. Again Ben winced.

"Oh hell, I'm sorry. Been meaning to get that fixed. Finish your hooch. I have to test your noggin. See if it's still in working order, bell or no bell.

"How many fingers am I holding up? Count backwards from ten. Tell me when my finger becomes double. What's my name? What's your name? Where's your horse?"

"How am I doing?"

"One out of six. Not bad." He started his cackle. But mercifully cut if off.

"Can I get up?"

"Give it a day or two. Wait till the pain's completely gone. In the meantime, relax. Enjoy yourself. You look as if you could use a vacation. Hungry?"

"Not too . . ."

Wysock consulted his watch. "It's five past ten. Do yourself a favor, try and sleep. If you're still awake around noon we'll feed you. Otherwise, you can sleep through. Sleep is what you need most of right now."

• • • •

She was close to six feet tall standing in her beaded moccasins. Slender waist; body bountifully, spectacularly contoured. She was beautiful, with dark, luminous eyes; obsidian ovals with light behind them. Her skin, too, was dark. As smooth as a baby's and as flawless.

She wore her sleek black hair in a single braid. It lay over her left shoulder and fell to her waist. She wore a white silk dress. Had it not been so plain, it might have served as a wedding gown.

She was perhaps the most striking woman Bert Slaughter had ever seen. She introduced herself as Maria Oloya Rodrigues Stewart. One-wife of Timinos, Howling Wolf. Split-Eye, Chief of the Mimbres Apaches. One-wife. An allusion not lost on Bert. Informing him as it did that the tall one was a one-wife husband. Something of a rarity among tribal chieftains.

They had been herded into a wickiup upon arriving. She was their first visitor. The *rancheriá*, more specifically a *choson*, the Aravaipas' word for hideout, was situated high in the Burro Mountains. Nearly seven hours journey from the place where Cutler had camped the night before. Of the twelve men under his command, counting Bert, eight had survived. One of the wounded had died on the way to the *choson*.

They had been escorted there with wrists tied in front of them. Sticks shoved over the crooks of their arms behind their backs. Forced to walk without stopping in blistering heat. Without water. They were utterly exhausted.

Cutler had become very talkative. Out of fear for his scalp. But had learned to curb his tongue. A sharp blow across the back of his neck with a lance shut him up. Bert enjoyed seeing him disciplined. He trudged along behind him. He chided him, laughed at him. Pleased that he'd now been reduced to his level. His equal. His upper hand dropped, and for good, from all appearances.

All eight of them were in the same boat now. It was leaking; it would eventually sink.

The woman spoke sharply to the two braves who had come in with her. Each carried a number of turtle-shell cups. each cup contained a different color paint. The braves untied them. The tendons in the crooks of Bert's arms were very sore. He flexed his arms to ease the discomfort and restore circulation. He kept his mouth shut. Not so Culter; he whined and complained and appealed for sympathy.

"Hold you tongue, white-eye," said Maris icily. "If you want to keep it. Or would you prefer it cut out. Strung on a pice of rawhide and hung around your scrawny neck?"

"I didn' say nothin'. 'Scuse me."

Bert snickered. Cutler glared. Maria leered.

"Ma'am," said Arthur Todd. "I don' want you should cut out my tongue, but I got to tell you. These fellas got no right takin' us prisoners. B'sides which the Army is out lookin' for us. They been trackin' us close. They'll pick up our trail easy. They'll come up here an' wipe you out. Women, children, all."

"You lie. Howling Wolf and his warriors watched you leave Las Palomas. You fled the town like scalded hounds. Like thieves in the night. No one followed you."

"You tell 'em, lady." Bert snickered.

"Shut up!"

She froze Cutler with a scowl. "*Chomata taree anda.* Sit still and be silent. No one will be harmed. *Chomata cota abisis.*"

She knelt before Cutler. She dipped her finger into a shell cup filled with yellow paint. And daubed an "x" on his forehead. He did not protest, did not budge. A brave crouching, holding his knife against his throat, discouraged him from either.

Bert smiled. He nodded approval at her choice of colors for him. He himself was painted a light blue. Each man received a different color. He sifted through his meager store of knowledge of Apache rites and rituals. He had no idea why they were being painted. And knew better than to ask.

Cutler didn't. Response to his question was her withering scowl. The brave holding the knife set the point against his Adam's apple. He pricked him lightly. A single bead of blood glistened.

She stared deep into his eyes. "The next time you speak. One word. One syllable, you will lose your tongue."

He swallowed. He clamped his lips tightly like a small boy. She dismissed the braves. She sat on the ground in front of them. She drew her knees up and tucked her long gown under her thighs holding the material in place with her long legs.

"We know that you are a pack of coyotes. Preying on your people. Stealing. Murdering. You . . ." She pointed at Cutler. "You are the leader. To us you are dirt. A whimpering dog. What you do to the white-eyes is of no interest to Howling Wolf. We have brought you here for a purpose." She touched her finger to her forehead. Indicating the x's on each of theirs. "A high and honorable purpose."

Bert looked askance at Cutler. He could see his lips formed the question "What?" but he did not speak. He'd been warned; he knew better.

"You do not know Timinos. Howling Wolf. My husband, Chief of all the Mimbres. You would not know him. We have been many years in the mountains to the south. But you should know that he is the son of Eskiminzin."

Bert started. A chill struck the nape of his neck. Lancing through the stifling air in which they sat. Eskiminzin. Apache of Apaches. Chief of the Aravaipas. Short, compared to Howling Wolf, very. Short and fat. But a warrior-leader on a par with Geronimo. With Mangas Colorados.

The many tribes of the Apache represented a scale of attitudes toward white-eyes. There were those who were friendly. As close as brothers to the white soldiers. Scouting for them. Wearing their uniforms; bearing their arms. Fluent in their language. Their purpose, vengeance against their own people for real or imagined offenses. And seeing the bluebellies as their most reliable allies.

Most of the tribes kept their distance from the white man. Some had little enmity toward him. Others clashed with him on occasion. And despised him. Still others fought him without letup. Keeping blood in their eyes and venom in their hearts against him.

At the top of the scale sat Geronimo. Cochise, Victorio, Nana, and a handful of others. Haters all. Blood foes. And above these was the squat, roly-poly Eskiminzin.

He had not always been consumed with hatred for white-eyes. He became so through a sequence of events; in their way they told the whole sad story of White-Indian relations in the West in the 19th century.

Eskimizin was originally a Pinal Apache. He married Aravaipa and joined her tribe. He became the leader of about 150 men, mostly Aravaipas; with a few Pinals. He and his people had no home. They had grown tired of fighting; they wanted a permanent peace with the Americans.

An army lieutenant, a man with a heart and intelligence, advised Eskiminizin to locate near Camp Grant in Arizona. The army would afford them protection from hostile white men. Presumably. Eskiminzin and his people took the lieutenant's well-intentioned advice. Soon their numbers increased to 500. The Indians spent their time gathering hay for the army post. Some hired out to nearby ranchers. One rancher, Charles McKinney, who lived on the San Pedro River, became a close friend of Eskiminzin. The chief often visited him. The two men enjoyed each other's company.

But the tribe's ever-increasing numbers worried the white residents of nearby Tucson. A group of citizens decided to take action. They recruited a force of about 50 Mexícans. And nearly a 100 Papagos Indians, longtime enemies of the Apaches. Unbeknownst to the Army, the combined force marched to the tribe's *rancheriá*. Shortly before sunrise they poured into the area from three sides. They massacred the unsuspecting savages. The Papagos wielded their knives and war clubs with devastating results. They crushed the skulls of the defenseless Aravaipas. They splattered their brains on the ground. They raped, mutilated, and killed young girls. Those who survived and tried to escape were cut down by the fire of the Mexicans and Americans. They had stationed themselves on a bluff overlooking the camp.

Eskiminzin was one of the few who escaped. He had awakened, grabbed his youngest son, and run. His two wives and five other children were killed. The fight, if such it could be called, was over in about half an hour. The Mexicans and Americans walked through the *rancheriá*, shooting the wounded. They set fire to the wickiups. They collected twenty-eight children prisoners and started back to Tucson.

The few survivors tried to rebuild the *rancheriá*, but the future was clouded. On one occasion a cavalry patrol from Camp Apache came upon them. They foolishly fired on Eskiminzin and his friends. Their aim was poor; no one was hurt. Eskiminzin was able to explain that he and his people were friendly. And were under the protection of nearby Camp Grant.

But the incident sickened him. The Army seemed incapable of protecting the Aravaipas. He decided that his only course was to drive all white men from the territory. Peace between their people and his was impossible.

Before leaving the *rancheriá,* he went to his old friend Charles McKinney one last time. McKinney greeted him warmly; he invited him for supper. They enjoyed their meal together. They talked and laughed; they recalled fond memories of their close friendship. But when the time came for Eskiminzin to leave, he drew his pistol. He shot McKinney through the head. And left him where he fell.

He explained to his people that he had not wanted to kill his friend. He had only done so as an object lesson for them. To teach them that there could never be friendship between them and the white man.

Said he, "Anyone can kill an enemy. It takes a strong man to kill a friend."

He had made his point. He led his warriors on one of the bloodiest warpaths in American history. Now his son was preparing to lead the sons of those warriors. Down the same trail.

Eskiminzin's story, his warm friendship with Charles McKinney and McKinney's murder, were well known throughout Arizona and New Mexico. Bert had often heard it. He wondered if the sequel soon to begin would be told as often in the years to come. One thing he could be sure of: neither his name or Cutler's would be remembered. They were merely pawns in the game. Howling Wolf's game.

Based upon the legacy of hate of Eskiminzin. His father.

Food was brought to them. A sour-tasting corn mush, raw badger meat, water, and a jug of *tiswin*. Enough to go around. But weak in alcoholic content. Too weak to take the edge off their dread. Bert was dying for a real drink. The nerves in his neck were tightening. He could be sure that the blue x painted on his forehead was to be his pass into the next world. That Cutler and the others also had their passes didn't made it any easier.

So he was to be killed. How? Suspended from a tree limb, hands tied behind his back? Over a fire that would boil his brains in the pot of his skull? Skinned alive for the amusement of the women and children? Given to the women to beat, burn, bludgeon, stone to death?

Maria Oloya Rodrigues Stewart went away. Leaving them free to talk without fear of losing their tongues. Words gushed from Cutler. As if his mouth had been corked and they had been building up in his brain. All questions. With no pauses between to permit answers. Though neither Bert nor anyone else seemed disposed to answer him.

"We gotta get away," said Cutler.

He had moved to the opening. He peered out. Bert had no notion of the time, but guessed it to be early afternoon. The shadow of a pinõn pine a few feet from the opening lay short on the ground, establishing that the sun had not wandered too far down from its zenith.

"We'll wait till dark. Then . . ., then . . ."

Cutler turned and looked to Bert for help.

"Then."

"Shut up, I'm thinkin' . . ."

"Don' strain yourself."

"How'd you like me to bust every bone in your body?"

"I'd purely love you to try."

"Aw c'mon." Arthur Todd shoved his way between them. "Let's not squabble 'mongst ourselves, please? We're all in the same boat. We should be workin' together." He eyed Bert. "Got any idees?"

"You bet. My head's crawlin' with 'em. How about we rush 'em? Slap 'em dizzy, then kill 'em with rocks."

"Shut up! Can't you see he's mockin' you, Arthur Todd? How stupid can you be? What are you, R.B.?"

"R.B.'s dead, Rance." said another man.

"He should be. A hunnerd times over. We can thank him for us bein' here!"

"Let's not give him all the credit," said Bert. "We'd be here even if he didn't go off half-cocked."

"You don' know that. YOU DON' KNOW NOTHIN'!"

"I know one thing. You shoulda' given it to me las'

night. Now your chance is by the boards. You'll likely die before I do."

"They're not gonna' kill us," said Donald. "If they was, they woulda' already. Wouldn' they?"

Bert fixed him with a jaundiced look. "You askin' or tellin'?"

"Well, wouldn' they?"

"You're a caution, Donald . . ."

"Don' nobody listen to him," said Culter. "I say he don' know nothin' an' he don't."

"I can put two an' two together. They didn't gussy us up with this paint, every man a different color for Hallowe'en. They didn' do you to take attention away from that disgustin', ugly lookin', cut-out eye o' yours. I mean that's ug-lee. Makes you homely as a damn mud fence, you know that? You should see yourself. Ugly, scared, practically shakin' in your boots. Look at him sweat, boys. Take a good look at your peerless leader. Ain' he somethin' to behold? Gettin' a littler hard to hold your bowels in check, Rance? Is it?"

Cutler lunged at him. Bert sat with his elbows atop his upraised knees. He threw himself backward. Up came his arms stiffening. He caught Cutler full in the gut with his right foot. Sent him flying over him. Crashing in a heap behind. Bert sprang up.

"Come on, you one-eyed son of a Chinese whore! Come get the thrashin' o' your life!"

"Bastard . . ."

Donald and Arthur Todd pushed between them.

"Cut it out!"

Cutler dropped his hands. He glared viciously. Bert laughed.

Outside, the shadow of the pinõn pine lengthened. The sun set. Darkness settled over the *choson* of Howling Wolf and his people. Maria came into the wickiup. She was followed by two braves. In her hand was a small clay bottle.

"Sit, everyone. SIT!"

She crouched before Donald. He sat in the forefront of the group.

"Everyone quiet."

All eyes were on her. She held the bottle up and shook it. Its contents rattled. Slowly she tipped it down. A single stone tumbled out. It was green. It matched the color on Arthur Todd's forehead. He did not seem to realize it at first. Not until the others turned and stared at him. He stared back bewildered. She restored the stone to the bottle. And nodded to the braves in turn. They grabbed Arthur Todd; they lifted him to his feet.

"What are you doin'? Whatsa matter? Hey . . ."

"Come along."

"Where?"

Fear vised him. His normally flushed cheeks turned ashen. He gulped and wide-eyed her. He was terror stricken.

"Why me?"

"Your color. Green. Bring him."

They watched him dragged outside. He struggled, pleading, screaming. No one else uttered a sound. Maria followed them out. Donald scurried to the opening and peered out.

"They're taking him up into the woods. What for, do you think? Why'd they take him, Rance? He didn't do nothin' . . ."

"You heard her. You saw his color come up." Bert nodded.

Ten minutes passed. The sounds of drums began; it drifted down through the woods to the wickiup. It entered Bert's ears; it invaded his brain. It magnified to a crescendo, keeping perfect rhythm with the thundering of his heart.

Maria did not come back to tell them what was going on. There was no need.

• • • •

Doctor Wysock kept Ben in bed. He passed the time browsing through medical books. Between bouts of worry about Bert. Before his horse threw him, before the lights went out a hunch was building in his breast. He was getting close to Bert. He would catch up with him before the day was out. With or without Cutler.

The impression was vividly clear. The next thing he knew, he was flying through the air.

By the middle of his second day in bed he was fed up. He would leave as soon as Wycock left for the day. Around six in the evening. But when he left, Ben made a discouraging discovery. He was able to get out of bed but standing upright on his rubbery legs triggered dizziness. In seconds the room was whirling. A carrousel running out of control. He nearly fell; he staggered his way to the nearest wall. Back came his headache with a vengeance. He slid down the wall, sitting on the floor. He breathed slowly, deeply. The room slowed to a stop. The aching in his head eased; it went away. Back into bed he crawled.

He slept that night without pain. Wycock came in at seven in the morning. With him was a patient; he had been shot in the arm in a fight at the saloon. Wysock sat him in a chair, dug out the slug, washed and bandaged the wound. The man paid him a dollar and left. Ben watched it all from his bed. After the man left, Wysock served him his breakfast. Then he removed his bandage. He examined his head. Ben felt no pain. There was no dizziness.

Wysock announced that if Ben stayed free of pain for the next three days, he would release him. He was to take it easy, however; he was not to ride his horse. The doctor seemed to think that letting him go two days before his week was up would be helpful. Ben hadn't the heart to tell him otherwise. Five days away from the chase was as bad as seven.

Wysock left the office early in the afternoon to deliver a baby. Ben got up a second time. He sat on the bed fully fifteen minutes before he tried to stand. When he did he did not move for another fifteen. His patience paid off. He felt no pain. Experienced no dizziness.

He left. He paid for his horse, mounted slowly, carefully, and rode off.

• • • •

Maria reappeared with her bottle of pebbles, an hour after nightfall the second night. The prisoners shrank back in a body at sight of her. She leered. Howling Wolf came in behind her. So tall was he, he had to lower his head to avoid hitting the ceiling.

"Look at them, husband. Look at their faces. We are not welcome."

"Whatja do with Arthur Todd!"

Cutler's sudden burst of resentment surprised Bert. He eyed him.

She turned to Howling Wolf and spoke. He went out. He came back in immediately carrying a heart. Human. It dripped with blood. Bert took one look, wished he didn't, and lowered his eyes to the ground. But could still smell it. Or imagined he could. His stomach made no such distinction.

"He returns to you," said Maria. She tittered. "You don't recognize him? See, husband, they cannot bring themselves to look. Are these the brave warriors whose blood and strength and courage we blend with our young men's? Is this the best we can do? It is pointless. Stupid! Pato, the shaman, uses rabbits when mountain cats are needed!"

"*Charma cooga enmosa!*"

Whatever he said put her in her place. She flashed a sheepish look at the ground. Then she knelt and picked up the dripping heart. She held it high. Moving it left and right in the matter of a turkey platter presented for the approval of hungry diners.

"Your friend. Your companion. In death he serves his fellow man more than he ever did in life. More than he ever expected to. His death was honorable. Be proud of him. In a way, if it please you to think it, he has expiated your sins. The sins of all white-eyes against our people. *Manacha*!"

Howling Wolf called outside. A squaw entered. She took the heart from Maria's dripping hands and went back out.

"It will be buried in the mound of one of our fallen warriors. He will sleep with two hearts. Even the heart of a rabbit has some courage to add to his own. Do you understand? Any of you? It serves a double purpose. To empower our youth *and* our dead. Place your hands against your chest. Feel your own hearts pound in appreciation for the high purpose that awaits them."

Howling Wolf withdrew. Maria picked up her bottle. She raised it for all to see, lowered and tilted it. Out fell a single pebble. Light blue.

Bert swallowed and sighed.

Nine

In a clearing in the woods lay a flat stone approximately fifteen feet across. Four stakes were driven into the ground at the corners. A long piece of rawhide was tied to each stake. It trailed onto the stone, the four free ends touching at the center. The stone was spattered with dried blood. Young boys clad in breechclouts and headbands only stood in a silent circle around the stone. They carried no weapons. Bert was pushed into the clearing. Atop tall poles torches flickered, coppering the boys' expressionless faces.

One boy's entire body was painted the identical light blue daubed on Bert's forehead.

So this was Howling Wolf's fresh young army-to-be. In noble obedience to his father's will. Eskiminzin's command that he dedicate his life to destroying white-eyes. Bert studied the painted boy. Before the North Star reached the next hour in its journey around the Big Dipper, the boy would be drinking from *his* heart.

He looked skyward. As he did so, a single raindrop struck his upturned cheek. Turbid black clouds swam the heavens. Crashing silently against one another. He was preparing to lower his eyes when lightning split the clouds jaggedly. Bluing the gathering; setting the specks of quartz in the surface of the stone gleaming brightly. Briefly. Thunder grumbled.

The rain started. Once more the sword of lightning ignited the sky. Again the thunder spoke. Howling Wolf and Pato the shaman, a withered, sickly looking little man were talking in low tones. Pato looked like a wrinkled toad. The two sat cross-legged on the far side of the stone.

It was the shaman's show. All tribal rites and rituals followed his dictates. The rain fell harder. The boys stood as still as the trees behind them. The scent of pine filled the air sweetly; Bert sucked in a deep breath; it failed to soften the hammering of his heart. Howling Wolf pointed at him. He spoke. The two braves who had brought Bert from the wickiup pushed him down onto the stone. They spread-eagled him. They tied his wrists and ankles; they ripped off his shirt.

What a crazy way to get his ticket punched, he thought, Bizarre, excruciatingly painful; much too slow; it presented all the worst aspects of dying. One following hard after another. All thanks to Cutler. No. This was his own doing. If he hadn't chased after him. If he hadn't messed up, gotten too close, carelessly let himself be caught. If, if, if . . .

He turned to look at Howling Wolf and the shaman. The old man handed the chief a knife. It was fully a foot long. It gleamed in the torchlight. The boys stared straight ahead. Seemingly without seeing, so blank were their faces. Bert glanced at the painted boy.

You're getting a good heart, he reflected wearily. Maybe not the best; far from it. Not free of sin. Not the bravest, but guts enough to get by all these years. An honest heart.

And healthy. Fair . . . The rain was washing the boy's paint off. His own left eye stung slightly. As the paint on his forehead streamed down into the inner corner.

So Howling Wolf would do the honors. He was in for a surprise. When he plunged the knife home, when he severed the main artery, his heart would jump two feet in the air. It was pounding so. Jump and fly away; they'd be no more able to grab hold of it than kids snatching at a greased pig at a fair. He'd die happy. In pain, but happy. Maybe not happy, but with a little warm gloat of satisfaction.

It pounded and pounded. He looked down his bare chest. He could see it battling to break out. Down past it his stomach twitched. Fear sent nausea creeping into it. Howling Wolf's shadow fell across him. In his grip was the knife, poised inches above his heart. He slowly raised the knife. Bert took a deep breath. He closed his eyes. He'd have to feel it, but he wouldn't have to see.

Lightning flashed through his sealed lids. It struck; it stabbed a tree outside the circle of boys. With a great crackling sound it fell; smashing down upon the blue boy. Crushing, killing him instantly.

Bert had opened his eyes as the lightning struck. He saw the tree fall and crush the boy. Howling Wolf too saw. Everyone did. A loud gasp ran through the gathering. Only Howling Wolf did not react. Nor did his expression alter in the slightest. He returned his attention to his task.

But Pato had sprung to his feet. He shouted and gesticulated. And bounded up onto the stone. He grabbed the chief by the arm. The boys had broken ranks. They tugged at the fallen tree to move it off the dead boy.

Pato and Howling Wolf argued. Bert held his breath. The rain fell harder. Now they were shouting at each other. The shaman was like a wild man. He pointed at Bert; he waved his arms; he jumped up and down, his bare feet slapping the stone. Howling Wolf threw down the knife in disgust. On Pato's order Bert was cut free.

He got to his feet. He was shaking; sweat poured from him. Howling Wolfe glared at him. Pato pointed to the woods. Bert needed no second invitation. He ran. Past the boys struggling with the tree. Through the trees circling the clearing. Picking up speed; flying over the needle carpet, branches slapping him, his body, his face. On and on he ran through the gauntlet of the woods. He tripped over a log. He fell hard; he struggled to his feet and ran on.

He did not look back.

Ten

It was an argument between them that gave Ben more insight into how his father felt about him than any other. Actually, little more than a heated discussion. It took place just after Ben turned nineteen. He was home from college for the summer. Bert had come home from work to find him practice shooting. Sticking playing cards in the splits of the rail fence. Potting them from thirty feet. Trying to. Missing most. Up strode Bert red-faced and puffing. He wrenched the gun from his hand.

"Whatta ya think you're doin'?"

"What does it look like?"

"Why? What for? You're educated. Whatta ya need with firearms?"

"Who knows? I might be called upon to defend myself against a jealous classmate. Maybe at graduation. In the midst of their heaping all sorts of honors on me."

Bert did not explode in response. Instead he softened his scowl and tone.

"I've raised you to be a gentleman. With breedin' an' class. Educated. Everythin' I'm not, nor ever could be. This thing's a tool o' my trade. But it's not gonna be any tool o' yours. You'll be in a job that takes brains. No gunslingin'; no narrow 'scapes, riskiness . . ."

"Oh stop it. You're the agent in charge of the Rawlings depot. What gunslinging and narrow escapes do you run into?"

"I've run into my share in my time. And will again. I don' intend to be a agent the whole rest o' my life. The day after you graduate, I'm puttin' in for a detective's job. Oh yes, the company's got itself its own detective force now. John J. Valentine sent a letter 'round to all the offices tellin' as how Wells Fargo is sick an' tired o' bein' plagued with holdups. He's hired a man who can stop 'em. Name o' James B. Hume. Easterner. Noo York. He was marshal in Placerville in California. Sheriff o' Eldorado County, an' warden at the state prison in Carson City."

"Give me back my gun. There's three shots left."

"You're just wastin' good ammunition. Whyn'cha stick to throwin' rocks?"

"Give me the gun, dad."

"All right, all right, Mr. Too-big-for-your-britches! Here. Let me see you hit somethin'. Just take care you don' kill any neighbors. I hate makin' enemies outta' carelessness. Hit the top spot on that deuce o' clubs. Go ahead . . ."

"Watch me . . ."

Ben aimed, fired, missed. Bert sniffed. He snatched away the gun. He fired twice. Destroying both spots cleanly.

"Let's go inside an' have us some supper. I been workin' all day, I'm hungry."

• • • •

Ben grinned. The turquoise sky appeared to have drained away all the sun's heat. Become itself a sun. It poured its fury down from every angle into every corner. It was like riding through a blast furnace. He took off his straw hat, and wiped his brow with his sleeve. He was still weak, but not dizzy; his head did not ache, but was sore where the road had hammered it. A bump had developed.

He had no idea how far he had come from Las Palomas. He jerked the reins, heeled the horse, picked up the pace. A large jagged outcropping surrounded by cactus caused a bend in the road ahead. He held his breath as he did at every turn. And trotted into and through it.

To his left were signs of a campfire. The fire itself was long dead. As were three men close by. He recognized them. They had helped to blow the safe in Fruitland. Cutler was not among them; more importantly, neither was Bert. The one he remembered Cutler calling R.B. looked like a pin cushion. He counted eighteen arrows in his chest. He got back on the road and went on.

He rode almost twenty minutes more before spotting a figure. A man lying face down in the ditch. He galloped forward; his heart climbed into his mouth; nervous sweat burst from him.

Bert. No mistaking that back. Down to his battered and scarred Frye boots. He was stripped to the waist. His face was buried in his hat. He was dead.

He galloped up to where he lay; and threw himself from the saddle.

"Oh, dad. Oh, God. I knew it, I knew it. Godddddd . . ."

Bert grunted. Ben started; his jaw dropped. Bert turned his face out of his hat and one-eyed him.

"Knew what?"

"You're alive!"

"The hell I am. If I am, it's no damn thanks to you. Want to know somethin'? The gospel truth? The most terrible hardest thing for a father to take in this terrible life is knowin' he's got a son who lets him down. It's downright cruel. I hope with all my heart you'll never know the feelin'. I sure never let my daddy down. Not once. I was always there at his beck an' call. Where he went I followed. Just far 'nough behind to give him breathin' room. Not far 'nough to lose him. I used my instincts; I got great instincts. Pity you didn' inherit even a little speck . . ."

Bert sat and sighed and looked at him. "Why don't you stop it?"

"I'm serious. Seriously. A son lettin' his father down makes a man wonder where did I go wrong? I never once let my daddy down . . ."

"Just shut up."

"That's somethin' else. Wicked hard for a father to take. A son that's all the time sassin' him. Tellin' him shut up."

"What in God's named happened?"

"Nothin' much." Ben picked up his hat and lay it on his back. "Whatcha do that for?"

"To spare you a little sunburn. You're going to be boiled like a lobster. Roll over. Sit up."

"What the hell am I, a dog?"

"Where's your shirt?"

Bert enlightened him in brief. The effort proved too much for him. The last traces of stamina deserted him. Ben saw it coming. His heart went out to him.

"You need a doctor."

"Horseshit!"

Bert hadn't the strength to struggle against his picking him up. Ben stood him upright; he lifted him onto the bay's rump. Bert didn't have the strength to prevent it. But his mouth continued in good working order. As powerful as ever.

• • • •

Ben was not surprised. Doctor Wysock was very annoyed with him for leaving. He reamed him out in a few words, then turned his attention to Bert. By the time Ben had gotten him upstairs to the office, his father had made a miraculous recovery.

"I'll give you some salve to rub on your back," said Wysock. "It'll take the heat out. It's already starting to bloom. I'll give you a shot of popskull; it's about all I can do. Brother, you've got the constitution of a bull buffalo!"

"Comes from clean livin'."

They left ten minutes later. Bert wore a clean shirt given him by Wysock. They sat in the Las Palomas New York Restaurant alongside the biggest potted palm in the place. Bert ordered three steaks. One for Ben.

"We gotta eat fas' an' get back onto this thing. Time's wastin'..."

Ben stared as if he couldn't believe his ears.

"Gotta get back to that *choson*. An' grab Cutler. Get him outta' there b'fore tonight. His color could come up next, you know. It'd be jus' my luck it does."

"Can I ask you something? Do you ever bother to listen to what you're saying? Let alone think before you say it?"

Bert sniffed and crammed his mouth full of steak.

"Think for one minute. You chase Cutler. You catch him. Rather he catches you."

"That was jus' a bad break..."

"He's preparing to punch your ticket when the Indians arrive. You're both captured, your color is picked and by a major miracle, I mean a miracle that makes the parting of the Red Sea pale in comparison, you get away by the skin of your three good teeth. Now, having landed safely in my arms, you want to turn right around and go back. Walk straight back into the lion's mouth."

"Oh hell, I know it's risky..."

"Risky? IT'S SUICIDE!"

"Sssh, everybody's lookin'. Why you always gotta embarrass me?"

"Don't do it. Please I warn you, I won't let you."

"You're 'fraid, right?"

"Thank God I've brains enough to be."

"We're talkin' 'bout Cutler, remember? Reco'nize the name? Have you forgot what he did?"

"Of course not."

"I had him. Then he got me. Then they got us an' him an' me was back even. I got away, usin' my wits. He's still back there. I know where, an' I'm goin' after him. An' you're comin' with me."

"Not a chance."

Bert screwed up his face, mouthful and all. He prepared to drop acid in response. In walked Doctor Wysock.

"Hello, again. I spotted you through the window. Elinor Forbes over at Western Union got a wire for you, Ben. She was going to give it to the Wells Fargo agent for you, but she knew you were my patient . . ."

"Give it here," said Bert.

"For Ben."

"It's for us both. I'm the senior member o' the team. Give it here."

KC GROUP ARRESTED HELD FOR TRIAL STOP DROP EFFORT TO APPREHEND RC ET AL STOP INCREASING VOLUME CASES DEMANDS VB CASE BE OFFICIALLY CLOSED STOP LEAVE AT ONCE TUCSON STOP UPON ARRIVAL AGENT WILL EXPLAIN ASSIGNMENT

JBH

"Thank you, Doctor," said Ben. "Thank you from the bottom . . ."

"You b'lieve this!" Wysock stared in pretended shock and withdrew. "You know whose doin' this is? Not Hume's. Oh, I know you think him an' me got no use for each other. He calls me reprobate an' I call him stuffed shirt an' sermon-mouth an' such. We got our ups an' downs, maybe. But high up an' deep down we respects each other.

"This ain' him. Not by a long shot. It's that sneaky little wolf in snake's clothin', Tevis, that's who. I never could cotton to him. Those eyes o' his are like to freeze you in your boots. Son of a bitch's snakier than Jay Gould. He stole Wells Fargo, you know. Jerked it right out from under Henry Wells' an' Bill Fargo's unsuspectin' feet!"

"Orders are orders."

"Whatta you lookin' so all-fired pleased about?" Bert crumpled the telegram savagely and slammed it into the potted palm. "You think this is gonna stop me from goin' back after Cutler? Think again!"

"Orders are orders."

"Stop sayin' that! Look, what if we never got this. What if your funny-lookin' friend with the straw hair never come in here. Never found us? What if he come in ten minutes after we left town? Two minutes? One . . . ?"

"He didn't."

"Hume don' know that. Nor Tevis neither. Will you cut out that infuriatin' ninny-grinnin' an' listen!"

"You listen. Finish eating. We'll go get you a horse and some kind of weapon. We'll head south for Hatch. We'll follow the Rio Grande down and board the train for Tucson."

"Not me . . ."

"Bert, be reasonable."

Bert was getting redder by the minute. He opened his mouth to speak; he caught himself. He smiled.

"Okay."

"What did you say?"

"I said okay. Whatever you want. You're right, orders is orders. All part o' the job. This steak's tough as hoof. I'm full anyhow. Pay the tab an' let's get outta' here. Go find me a horse an' iron. An' maybe a plug o' Battle Ax, while we're at it."

His change of heart was much too abrupt to be anything but phoney. Ben nodded, agreeing with this assessment. On jabbered Bert. All sweetness and light and professions of cooperation. Orders are orders are orders. Ben resolved that from here to Hatch, he would watch Bert like a hungry hawk eyeing a field mouse. Whatever he had up his sleeve would stay there. If need be, he would tie him to his horse. Tie him to his train seat.

If it was the last thing he did, he'd get him to Tucson.

Eleven

"Remind me when we get to Hatch to wire San Franciso for some money," said Ben, "we're getting a little short."

"Why not wait till you get to Tucson?"

"You mean till 'we' get there . . ."

"I mean you."

Momentarily distracted by a stubborn latigo strap, Ben had turned his back on his father. It was his first lapse in vigilance. His first mistake. And his last. Down came Bert's new secondhand Colt, butt first. Ben sighed and crumpled in a heap. Bert glanced about. He had timed it perfectly; nobody passing by outside the livery stable had seen a thing. The stable owner had gone out back on a fool's errand, dispatched by Bert. He glanced down at Ben.

"Sorry, son."

He led the roan outside, mounted, and rode away at a gallop. He assured himself that he hadn't hit Ben very hard; just hard enough to extinguish his lantern, not hurt him. Decent people don't go around smacking others hard enough to hurt. Not those recovering from concussions certainly.

Six hour later, just past midnight, he came within fifty yards of the *choson*. Close enough for him to see through the trees that it was deserted. Leading his horse, he walked among the wickiups and dead cook fires. Split-Eye and his people had left in a hurry; taking Cutler and the other prisoners with them? He wondered. If he didn't find their bodies, they probably had. He found a saber hilt, but no blade, and a couple of government-issue Spencers with broken bolts, enough to tell him that Arthur Todd's lie to Maria had been prophetic. The army had been after them. And had caught up at last.

Curiously, he could find no bodies. No Apaches. No bluecoats. No outlaws. He searched every wickiup. And found nothing other than signs of hurried departure. A few trees showed fresh slug gouges. But other than these, there were no signs of battle. Perhaps Howling Wolf had guards out. Far enough out to send back warning in time for everybody to get out.

He led the horse up the path to the flat stone. The rain had washed it clean of blood. He stared down at it. He pictured himself lying spread-eagled and tied. The circle of boys surrounding. The painted one. The struck tree lay close to where it had fallen. Moved just enough to get the boy's body out from under it.

Again he saw the torches burning, hissing as the rain struck them. He saw Howling Wolf and Pato. And the two braves who had tied him. It was all a bad dream dreamt years before; nothing about it seemed real.

He lost himself in reverie. He was tired; he had not slept since the night before last. He'd run most of last night. Until he reached the road, stumbled, and fell in the ditch. Where Ben had come upon him.

He heard the swishing of branches behind him. He jumped up and went to his gun. It was Ben. So vicious was his expression, Bert took a step backward.

"Easy, son.

"Easy he says. You could have killed me! I've got a concussion . . ."

"In the front. That's why I hit you in the back . . ."

"MY ENTIRE SKULL, YOU IMBECILE!"

"Aw c'mon, it was a love tap, light like a feather. I know how to hit somebody, I got it down to a science."

"I could wring your neck, deceitful bastard . . ."

"Tsk tsk tsk, such language."

"My horse is down below. Let's go. We can make Hatch before sunup if we get a move on."

"You go on ahead, I'll catch up . . ."

"Oh no you don't."

"In a minute then. It was a long haul up here. Let's just catch our breaths. This is where it all happened, son. The lightnin' hit that tree over there. Just as Howlin' Wolf was about to shove his knife clean through my heart. Hit the tree, the tree hit the boy. Talk about dumb luck, it was amazin', stupefyin'. A miracle. God send down a bolt o' lightnin' an' saved my life. He did. Nex' Sunday I'm goin' to church."

"Let's go."

"Wait, wait. I'm goin' an' give thanks."

"You haven't been inside a church in twenty years."

"It's never too late to pick up the traces. Tell you somethin' else, everytime I see a bolt o' lightnin' from now on, I'm gonna' thank it out loud for bein' in the right place at the right time. A miracle, that's what it was. I never in my life been closer to havin' my ticket punched. Suddenly, down she comes an' turns the whole shebang upside down. Busted the shaman's magic to bits. He wouldn' let Split-Eye go through with it. He saw the signs, knew the Great Spirit didn't approve, you know?"

"Come on. We can reminisce on the way."

"I'm goin' to church. Not jus' this Sunday, every Sunday. Nex' hotel we stop at I'll get me a Bible. Carry it on me wherever I go."

Moonlight filtered through the trees; it paled his sun-browned face. He nodded and nodded. "There's somethin' else, Ben. It come to me on the way here. You know how you get all the pieces of a puzzle, but no matter how hard you try they jus' don' seem to want to fit together? You know how that is? Well, I finally got 'em to fit."

"Good. Now could you get to the point?"

"The point is Cutler."

"He's probably dead."

"Don' bet on it. He coulda' got out; him an' his brood. In the middle o' the fracas here . . ."

"I don't see much evidence of any fracas. It looks to me like the Indians packed up and ran. Five minutes ahead of the troopers."

"An' took Cutler an' the others with 'em. An' he got away . . ."

"You're just guessing."

"Educated guess." He bit off a chunk of his plug; he chewed aggressively. "What I was gettin' at before about the pieces bein' him. The point. Let's say he did get away. Where do you think he'd head?"

"Mexico. Where else? I though we'd decided that long ago."

Bert poked his chest; his eyes gleamed. "You think so? I did b'fore. Not now. Go back to Leadville. They hit there, then headed south. Gunnison, Durango, Fruitland, down to Las Palomas."

"Exactly. Straight for the border. My guess is Cutler planned all along to cut his friends in Kansas City out completely. The best way of doing that would be to run down to Mexico and hide in the mountains. Get rid of his accomplices, get away from the law."

"I think he meant to, until he got to Las Palomas. The next mornin', when we were camped out an' Split-Eye showed up an' captured us, from that time on Cutler never once mentioned the money. Not a whisper. It was like he didn't have a worry in the world about it."

"What are you trying to prove? He had other things on his mind, like his life."

"Oh, he was worried they were gonna kill him; sure, weren' we all? But there at the camp, on the way to here, an' sittin' in the wickiup, all that time he never said a blessed thing 'bout the money. He talked about everythin' under the sun, except it. It was like it was safe someplace; *he* wasn', but it was. That made me start thinkin' back to Las Palomas. We had to kill time till dark, so we went an' had somethin' to eat an' killed a couple hours in the saloon. While we were sittin' drinkin', he suddenly got up an' him an' Donald an' a couple others, the older hands, went out the back door. He was carryin' the loot in his saddlebag over his shoulder; every penny. He left with it. He come back twenty minutes later; he was still carryin' it.

"But in that twenty minutes he stuck it someplace. For certain."

"That's just a wild guess."

"He did. Think about it. He had it all planned how he was gonna head for Mexico and cut out the Kansas City bunch, *an'* get away from us. He likely still means to."

"Didn't you just say . . ."

"What I'm trying to say is he hid the money someplace in town, him an' Donald an' those other two, *to cut out the rest*. So the four o' them could hog it all. You gotta understan', when he walked out the door with the three, the ones left were all greeners. Milk-fed babies fresh off the farm. I'd bet my life it was the first time on the owlhoot trail for every one. They trusted him, didn't dare cross him, wouldn' dare question him 'bout the money.

"Yes, sir, he stashed it in Las Palomas; an' he's comin' back for it."

"It sounds incredibly complicated. Full of holes. For example, what happened to his gang, the young ones? Won't they come back with him?"

"Oh hell, he'll shake them easy as a sidewinder sheds its skin. They trust him; he could send 'em down to the San Luis Pass into the Sierra Madres to wait for him. They'd do it, they're that green, that stupid. They'd wait till they drop dead o' old age. Meantime, he goes back, picks up the money, an' heads for wherever."

"Providing he gets away from Howling Wolf. If he doesn't . . ."

"He's dead. But I'll put my money on him. He's not what you call intell'gent, but he's shrewd as riverboat gambler. Son, you know me, I get gut feelins; this is one. I got to go with my gut. I see how the cards are fallin' clear as glass, honest. I *know* he's comin' back. Here's what we do, you go on to Tucson . . ."

"Bert . . ."

"Will you let me finish? I stay in Las Palomas, hang aroun' an' watch for him."

"The chances are nine out of ten he'll never show."

"My instinct say nine outta' ten he will."

"It's no good. Even if by some wild stroke of luck he does, he won't be alone. There'll be at least three or four with him. Maybe all. Which puts you back where you started. Outside of Fruitland; outmanned, outgunned . . ."

"I can take care o' me. I'll have surprise on my side."

"You had it before. For all the good it did you. I don't like it, it's leaky as a sieve."

"It's not!"

They argued for upwards of an hour. They sat on the sacrificial rock in the moonlight. Both fighting fatigue, working down to the raw ends of their nerves. Now and then flaring at each other. Every so often Ben would reach for the back of his head where Bert had hit him. As if to remind himself that he should be upset over it.

Trying to change Bert's mind about anything was like trying to talk a tree into moving out of the way. The man had written the book on stubbornness. And lived by it chapter and verse. Ben finally gave up.

"All right, go back to Las Palomas. Go back and sit like a toad on a rock. Wait a year and a day. He'll never show. Meanwhile, you'll lose your job. Hume's wire was very explicit. Drop the case, head for Tucson. There's some kind of high-priority shipment going out. We've been assigned to guard it. I'll be there; you won't."

"You don' need me. You can juggle six balls in the air at once. You're good, son. A first-rate detective. I'm proud o' you . . ."

"Oh, shut up!"

Bert looked hurt. "You should learn to take compliments gracious-like."

"I give you fair warning. When James Hume calls you on the carpet, don't look to me to jump in and defend you. Orders are orders. It's your job as much as mine to obey them."

"You make it sound like the army."

Ben stood up. "Go back if you like. I'm heading for Hatch."

"Good luck, son. I mean it sincerely. Aren't you gonna wish me some?"

"You're incorrigible. I don't know how I put up with you! You're not a partner, you're a millstone around my neck! I must have a martyr streak in me! I'm probably destined for sainthood!"

"You betcha. You're one of a kind. I'm proud of you . . ."

"Stop at a hotel and get a Bible. Incorrigible! Incredible! Good night!"

"Goodbye, son. *Vaya con Dios*. Sorry I busted your straw skimmer. I owe you one."

Ben grunted. A familiar sound. Bert liked it; he acquired a new trait. Inherited it. He smiled inwardly; like father like son.

Twelve

"Where's your partner?"

Agent Dillon Coopersmith was in charge of the Wells Fargo agency in Tucson. He displayed a barrel chest and the belly to support it. And the shoulders of a nine-year-old, all but absent on either side of his full beard.

They stood outside the office in the blazing sunlight. The heat did not appear to bother Coopersmith; Ben had had his fill of it. From Hatch, every mile westward seemed to raise the temperature a fraction of a degree. By the time his train arrived in Tucson he felt like water spilling from a barrel.

"My father's a sick man. He may need an operation. I left him in a little place north of Hillsboro. Back across the border."

"That's a shame. Serious, eh?"

"Very, when I left him. I hated to."

Lying warmed his cheeks. And raised his eyes slightly

in their sockets. Bert lied as effortlessly as he breathed; he had a gift for it. And was proud of it. Ever eager to display it. But it made Ben feel uncomfortable. Oh well, he reflected, somebody in the family had to have a conscience.

"You think you can handle this job alone? Course there'll be the shotgun messenger and the driver'll be armed . . ."

"What's it all about, Mr. Coopersmith?"

Ben glanced past him as he asked. Down the eastbound road. Fleetingly, wildly, vainly hoping he'd see Bert come dusting up it. But there was no dust, no sign of a soul. A wretched-looking hound made its way slowly across the street. It hung its head, the tips of its ears dragging in the dust. It looked as if it hadn't rained here since the flood. For a territorial capital, Tucson struck him as woefully primitive, all but completely lacking the telltale touches of modernity seen in most towns. A squalid heat collector, squatting on the Santa Cruz river 130 miles southwest of Phoenix. The surrounding country was dry and unproductive, except where it was irrigated. But the soil was reputedly rich, and the town served as the center of one of the oldest farming and ranching districts in Arizona.

It looked unimpressive. But it did boast the division headquarters and major repair shops of the Southern Pacific railway, and as a settlement, had been continuously occupied for nearly 200 years.

Ben's question drew a sly smile from Coopersmith. He winked and ushered him inside the office.

"Close the door and bolt it."

A stagecoach strongbox, painted the usual Well Fargo green, iron belted and with leather grips, stood in one corner. Coopersmith opened it. Ben felt his eyes tug in their sockets. The box was almost filled with neatly stacked, gleaming gold coins.

"Spanish doubloons . . ."

"Mexican, Mr. Slaughter. Each one worth sixteen silver dollars American. You're looking at almost sixty thousand dollars. Most valuable shipment I've sent out in fourteen years with the company."

"Whose are they?"

"Private citizen. She's shipping them to San Francisco."

"By stage?"

He shrugged. "It's her money, she can ship it by dog sled if she likes. I got instructions from the home office for you two, for you, that is. By the way, do you think you can handle a job this size on your own?"

You already asked that, reflected Ben.

Coopersmith accepted his nod and got out a bottle and a couple of tumblers. He wiped out each with his index finger. He held them up to the sunlight to appraise the job. His belly and his roseate-webbed eyes testified that he was a conscientious, two-fisted drinker. If Ben needed additional proof, his breath provided it. It smelled as if he'd been chewing on a bar rag. He downed his first glass in one herculean gulp, and poured a second with a trembling hand.

"Don't let me get too far ahead of you, soldier."

The doubloons, he explained, would not be traveling by strongbox. The strongbox would be filled with the usual letters, small parcels, and some money. The coach boasted a newly installed secret compartment four inches deep, artfully concealed beneath the floor.

"You could lie on your back under the coach, look up, and not see a thing. A holdup man could look for six hours and never spot it. Ingenious, eh?"

Ingenious and a slight exaggeration, mused Ben. A little rapping with a gun butt would elicit a hollow sound; still, anyone demanding of the driver that he throw down the box, seeing the ordinary green one landing at his feet, would be unlikely to look further.

"Who knows about this?"

"Wells Fargo people only. The driver, the shotgun messenger, you, and me."

"And the carpenter or carpenters who built and intalled the secret compartment?"

"Carpenters don't hold up stages, soldier."

"They can throw in with those who do."

He told him about the dynamite hidden in the Vollmer-

Bolton safe doors. Coopersmith reacted startled. He knew nothing about Rance Cutler's recent escapades at the expense of the company; he wouldn't, his office safe was an ancient Dumbrille. He hadn't received any warning letter from Hume.

"Drink up, soldier, you're getting behind."

Coopersmith poured his third drink in as many minutes and sat down to enjoy it. His blood splotched eyes were taking on a glazed look. Why, wondered Ben, did he bother with a glass? Why waste the time and effort? He sipped his own drink, purely out of politeness. It was vile stuff. It put him in mind of castor oil generously laced with kerosene. It bit, it burned.

"You got here just in time," said Coopersmith. "You'll be leaving seven o'clock sharp tomorrow morning. Four passengers, but only two through. You'll be picking up and dropping. The idea is to present an ordinary appearance, just another run."

"How far is it?"

"To Frisco? Better than a thousand miles. Eleven days."

"How many stops?"

"Every twelve to fifteen miles as usual. Every town of any size. All part of appearances. Any holdup types see or get wind of a stage moving through their territory nonstop, they're bound to get suspicious. Did I tell you this is the biggest shipment I've sent out in my fourteen years with the company?"

"You did."

"Like to see the drawn-up plan of the secret compartment? It's ingenious as hell. You lie on your back under the coach, look up at the floor, and you can't see a thing."

You told me that too, thought Ben.

He must have been something of a mind reader. He discarded his tumbler. And began tugging straight from the bottle. Then he turned to rummaging through the mass of papers atop his desk. Ben picked up a doubloon and examined it. On one side was King Philip's curly-wigged profile. On the reverse, His Majesty's royal crest. It bore the date 1736.

"Who'd you say these belong to?"

"A lady. I've never met her. She didn't arrange the shipment. Two fellows, her representatives, came in here about ten days ago. Big, strapping bozos. Mexicans. Or Mex-Indians. Both in expensive togs, pearl studs and all. Both spoke perfect English. They set everything up with us. Paid cash for the works. Including installation of the secret compartment."

He found the carpenter's plan. As he did so his eyes lit on another piece of paper.

"Here's the owner. Calls herself Maria Oloya Rodrigues Stewart. Quite a mouthful, eh?" Ben drew a breath in sharply. "You know her?"

"I've heard of her."

Thirteen

CAPTURED BY SAVAGES STOP I ESCAPED STOP FATHER STILL PRISONER STOP HAVE FOOL-PROOF RESCUE PLAN BUT NEED MONEY TO PURCHASE HORSE GEAR WEAPONS STOLE BY CAPTURERS STOP HURRY MATTER LIFE AND DEATH

BS

The Western Union clerk lifted her massive, gunmetal gray wigged head. And peered over her gold-filled spectacles at Bert.

"Isn't this word here stole*n*?"

"Whatever . . ."

"And captors. I don't think there's any such word as capturers."

"Whatever. Can you get it off pronto? I'm in a scaldin' rush."

"Right away. Thirty-five cents, please."

"Send it collect, please, all I got is a fifty-dollar bill. No small change."

"I can change a fifty."

"Good, but send it collect anyhow."

• • • •

SINCERELY HOPE RESCUE PLAN SUCCESSFUL STOP AVOID UNNECESSARY RISKS STOP SUGGEST ENLIST LOCAL ASSISTANCE STOP KEEP US INFORMED

JBH

"I'll do that," said Bert. He counted the fifty dollars a third time, but it stubbornly refused to increase in amount. "Cheapskates."

Outside the Western Union office he glanced across the street. He crossed and took up his vigil in the shadows in the alley alongside the livery stable. From this vantage point he could see the entire center of town, and up and down Main Street running east to west. He could not see north and south, the street bisecting Main, but decided that the chance of Cutler's coming in from the west, the direction of the Burro Mountains, was his best bet.

If he came riding in at all. He couldn't deny it was the longest of long shots. To begin with, it depended on Cutler's getting away. Not impossible, but far from easy. If he failed to, if he was killed trying, if he never even tried, none of the other pieces could fall into place.

One thing Bert was absolutely convinced of: the loot was hiding somewhere here in town. He had no proof of this. But his instincts insisted it was so. So if Cutler did get away, he would surely come back. How many would be with him was another question.

So many questions. So many conclusions inviting jumping to. So few answers.

"It's downright discouragin', Slaughter. Disgustin'. . ."

He was exhausted. But didn't dare steal time to sleep. If

Cutler was coming there no telling when. He could come loping in at two in the morning.

Bert slid his back down the side of the stable. He sat on the ground. He tried dozing with one eye open. It was impossible. The day wore on; the shadows stretched toward Texas. In time the sun began pulling in its cruel rays. Its whiteness gave way to yolk yellow. This in turn deepened to blood red. The burning air hung completely motionless. Not a single mote of dust rose in the street. Las Palomas slept.

He was thirsty. Up the street four doors, the batwing doors of the saloon beckoned. He was tempted to head for them. Steal five little minutes. Line his throat and infuse his life with enjoyment. And bring a bottle back. At five-thirty he did so.

He sat in the alley all night, taking only time out to eat. He sat in the window of the Las Palomas New York Restaurant so that he could keep an eye on the street.

He returned to his post. He slept sitting, permitting himself to slip into a doze. The initial level of sleep. From which the slightest sound would awaken him. And did. By morning, in spite of cat-napping, he was exhausted. His head ached furiously; his tongue had acquired a furry mitten; his upper eyelids felt as if they were lined with lead.

As his exhaustion increased, so, too, did his discouragement. All his wishful thinking appeared to be precisely that. His weary and throbbing brain went back to the sacrificial stone in the woods. His conversation with Ben. Ben's pessimism regarding his assumptions. About something else Ben had been right: Hume and Tevis would not take kindly to his ignoring orders. "We didn't get the telegram" was no acceptable excuse. Whenever he tried it, it wound up exploding in his face. The opening lie led to others. To contradictions. To a complete unraveling of the whole alibi.

Ben, too, worried him. He'd sent him off alone to Tucson. Into what? What sort of assignment? How dangerous? Without him there, Ben could get his ears blown off.

If that happened he'd never forgive himself. The dark side of the situation rose up suddenly like the shadow of death. It blocked out the sun. And plunged him deep into the pit of worry.

Still no sign of Cutler. Where had he hidden the loot? Bert's eyes traveled up the street past the Las Palomas Farmers & Merchants Bank. Past it one, two doors. Then returned to the bank.

"Hell, yes!"

Why not? What better place to stash it? The gold certificates and the securities he might not put in for safekeeping. His appearance would not work in his favor. He looked nothing at all like a man in honest possession of such paper. But anyone could deposit money in any bank. No questions asked. By God, if it was *him* it'd be exactly what he'd do!

But if Cutler did, why come back now?

Why not? Draw it out, stuff it back in his saddlebags, and head for the border.

There I go again, he thought irritably. Lining things up neatly. Orderly. Pretty as a picture. But with no real rhyme or reason. There I go again. He cursed wishful thinking. It was a trap he could never resist jumping into, despite all Ben's efforts and persuasion to prevent it.

Maybe the boy was right. Maybe he did have a slight tendency toward stubbornness.

• • • •

Ben ran his hand down the polished stock of his brand-new Winchester. He stood across the street from the depot. Watching the passengers board the stage: three men and a woman. She was young. His heart skipped a beat at his first glimpse of her. From a distance she looked amazingly like his mother in the photograph that Bert carried in his wallet. She came out of the office into the sunlight. Now the coach blocked sight of her. But in the few seconds he recognized the resemblance: the almost indentical shape of her face. The lovely dark eyes. Her chestnut hair.

The driver was already up on his box. The shotgun messengers closed the door and climbed up. Three men came running up. From Coopersmith's descriptions Ben recognized two as the well-dressed Mexicans who had arranged for Maria Oloya Rodrigues Stewart's shipment. The driver sat, reins in hand, waiting as they went inside. Moments later they came out and boarded.

So they were going along to keep an eye on the lady's fortune, were they?

The shotgun nodded to the driver. He slapped rumps. The Concord lurched away. Coopersmith, looking somewhat worse for wear, waved from the doorway. Mornings were hard on hard drinkers, mused Ben. He checked his watch: 7:02.

He watched dust collect behind the vehicle. He gave the driver a fifty-yard start. Then mounted up and followed. Coming out of the shadows into the early morning sun was something of a shock. The glare was fierce. Two hours later, before it had ascended even halfway to its zenith, the sun became as brutal as in New Mexico. As merciless. As tireless.

Ben had replaced his crushed straw hat with a Plainsman's hat. It was hotter than the straw. But less conspicuous. A man might as well display a fez as a straw hat in this part of the country.

He thought about the passenger and her striking resemblance to his mother. It stirred memories of that all-too-memorable birthday, her brutal murder, Cutler and Bert.

And Bert's present whereabouts. What was he up to? Had his wild long shot paid off? *Had* Cutler gotten away and come back to Las Palomas? He touched the bump on the back of his head. And regretted his failure to reciprocate in kind. He could have, slipping up behind Bert as he sat on the Mimbre's stone. Knocked him cold. Piled him on his horse tied hand and foot. Fetched him to Hatch. And from there to Tucson.

But he had not. Now 200 dusty miles separated them. With no possible means of contacting each other. He saw two choices: he could worry all the way to San Francisco. Or bar it from his mind.

He shifted his thoughts to Maria Stewart. From the little Bert had learned about her, it appeared she had run away from Mr. Stewart. And taken up with Howling Wolf. Wives ran off in the best of families. Though they didn't usually leave to go play wigwam with Indians. Least of all Apaches. Before she'd left, possibly after—sending word back to those she trusted—she had ordered $60,000 in gold shipped to San Francisco. He had noticed the destination on the shipping manifest when Coopersmith showed him her name. Someone called G. Roswell, Pacific Shipping Company, would be receiving. He had never heard of the company. He knew of many companies in town, but then there had to be at least sixty shipping firms semi-circling the bay.

Soapweed and brightly blooming acacias abounded. Agave, yucca, and a seemingly unlimited variety of cacti dominated by great columnar "chayas" were everywhere to be seen. The pungent odor of creosote bushes filled the sweltering air. Mesquite lent its dull gray and olive colors, harmonizing well with the rigidity of the forbidding barrenness of the plain. The enormous flower clusters of the yucca flaunted their loveliness. Pink and orange, crimson, yellow, and scarlet blooms of the giant cactus drew his eye.

The route followed the railroad tracks to Red Rock, Picachio, Arizola, Cas Grande, and Maricopa. There, near the River Reserve, the tracks curved left. They ascended into the Estrella Mountains. The stage deserted them; it took the right fork in the direction of the Gila River. Phoenix lay beyond.

It seemed unfair of Coopersmith not to tell the passengers about the gold under their feet. It did pose a danger to them, despite its being a closely guarded secret. Someone outside the company could have gotten wind of the shipment. Coopersmith had dismissed this possibility. But the Vollmer-Bolton case was still fresh in Ben's mind. Carpenters could be as greedy and dishonest as the people who assembled safe doors.

He dropped back an additional ten yards to ensure that anyone who saw them pass would not associate him with the coach. There was little traffic on the road. The few ranches that appeared were set well back from it.

• • • •

Bert slept almost the entire second night in the stable alley. He was simply too tired to stay awake. He woke up in the morning feeling wretched. Cursing. In need of a shave, a bath, a change of clothing. He continued cursing as he got to his feet, stretched, and toed into his Fryes. A woman passed by with two small children. She scowled. He cut off his foul mouth, but not quickly enough.

"He sounds like daddy," said the boy. He laughed. But stopped abruptly when his mother all but ripped his arm from the socket.

"Hush, Rupert!"

"Mornin'."

Bert tried for the friendliest tone he could muster. She froze him with ice blue eyes. On she walked with her two little ones.

"Sorry. Slip o' the tongue . . ."

He took his breakfast at the restaurant. At what had become "his" window table. After he had eaten he did not return to his post. Instead, trying to relieve his boredom, he took up his vigil across the street.

Four hours later he glanced up the street for the hundreth time. He blinked. He squeezed his lids tightly. Snapped them wide, gaped, and jerked his head back.

Cutler!

With him were the two older members of the gang.

"I knew it!" He chortled gleefully. And shook his fist at the gods. "I knew it! Knew it! Knew it!' I tol' ja, son. Didn' I? It had to be. Couldn' help but be! Watch 'em stop at the bank. Watch . . ."

They did so. And filed inside. Cutler carried his saddle-bags over his shoulder. Bert leaped in the air, barely suppressing a triumphal shout. Then suddenly stopped, puzzled.

Where in hell had Cutler found his saddlebags? The last he'd seen of them, they'd been riding the rump of Howling Wolf's pony.

He sneaked another look. They were all inside. He dashed across the street to his previous post in the stable alley. He ran down it and around the rear corner. He paid for his horse and went back to the alley. Their horses stood patiently at the hitch rack. He waited. Time crept by like a dying snake. For the first time in two days a breeze sprang up. It set a host of dust devils dancing in the street. He watched them perform, then settle themselves into the ruts of which they had risen. The mountain ridge under the sun to the west inched upward to meet it.

They came out at last. They were laughing, joking. Three honest businessmen making their withdrawal. A fat, vested, perspiring banker type appeared in the doorway. He waved them away.

Bert gave them two hundred yards before starting out. They rode toward Black Mountain. It rose north of the Burros, just beyond the Gila River. But long before they reached it, they turned even more sharply north. Minutes later they deserted the road. They cut through the tall grass. They pulled up at a small adobe house. It was surrounded by a picket fence in need of painting. They had approached the rear. The unseen front looked out on a narrow subsidiary road.

He dismounted and hobbled his horse. He left it to nibble grass. And himself dropped down into its protective cover. He moved forward on elbows and knees. Iron in hand, cocked and ready.

Someone was coming out to greet them. He recognized Donald. As far as he could see, he was the only greener left of the group. Another familiar face loomed behind his.

Bert gasped. "Mrs. Howlin' Wolf! I'll be jiggered!"

He watched in amazement as she greeted them smiling. Her smile said one thing: she was no prisoner. Cutler hadn't taken her as a hostage in his escape from the tribe. Had she helped him get away?

It didn't figure. Nothing figured at the moment. It was crazy. Like seeing a wildcat and a grizzly hail each other. Old home week. She had changed into a black dress with frilly cuffs and collar. Her hair was now in two braids instead of the one. But there was no mistaking her face. Or the beautifully formed rest of her.

"I've gone sun-daft. I got to be seein' things . . ."

He blinked and blinked. But he wasn't imagining it. There they stood, babbling away like old friends meeting. Delighted to see each other.

He watched all five disappear inside. He thought back to the wickiup. He pictured himself and Cutler and the others sitting helplessly as their foreheads were painted. Cutler she had singled out as the special target of her wrath. Threatened to cut his tongue out if he didn't shut up. The way she'd looked. The way she talked . . . Mere sight of him made her furious. He recalled as well the look she'd flashed him when Arthur Todd's color came up. And remembered thinking at the time she was disappointed that the yellow pebble hadn't tumbled out of her bottle. To match the color on Cutler's forehead.

Now here they were. Pleased as two lovebirds to see each other.

"Disgusin'!"

He holstered his gun. He rolled over on his back. And stared upward at the cloudless, turquoise sky. It was beginning to deepen in color as the sun approached its vanishing point.

What in the world had happened since the lightning bolt and his run for his life? Everything had turned upside down. Completely! What in boiling blue hell was going on?

Was she his hostage?

She couldn't be. She'd practically thrown her arms around him and kissed the greasy-haired son of a bitch! And how did Howling Wolf figure in it? Had he peddled her to Cutler for a mule and a plow? She wouldn't just up and run away. Not with a pig like Cutler.

What a shock! And her presence wouldn't make his job any easier. It promised tough enough to take out the three to get to him. With her on board . . .

"Of all the dumb, stinkin' turns!"

His reactions had run the gamut from shock to confusion to anger to grudging acceptance of the situation. He would wait till nightfall before deciding on his next move. In the meantime, he'd pull out all the pieces and try and fit them together. Try and make sense out of the thing. If he succeeded it would determine his strategy.

He snickered. Maybe what he ought to do was go out and find *Mr.* Stewart. Maybe he could explain his wife's weird turnabout. Ex-wife. Was she crazy in the head? She didn't act so. Her thinking in the wickiup was as clear as spring water. Her eyes looked perfectly sane. No question she despised Americans. And was intensely loyal to the chief, proud as a damned queen to call herself his "one-wife."

So why had she deserted him? Could it be that that was the way she played every man? Marry and run? No . . . Maybe . . . No. It was all so damned confusing! Why *had* she left Split-Eye?

Had she? Could it be that he'd been killed in the brush with the Army? Neither he nor Ben had seen a single corpse at the *choson*. Or anywhere near it. This didn't prove that nobody had been killed. But the absence of destruction, the paltry few slug gouges in the tree trunks, the fact that not even a dead horse could be seen lying about strongly intimated that the tribe had gotten out before the troopers arrived. Avoiding a bloodbath.

What happened after that, where the Indians had gone, and if the soldiers had ever caught up with them, were questions he couldn't possibly guess the answers to. Still, he'd put his money on the Mimbres; they knew the mountains, every foot, every tree. Along about now they probably had the troopers riding in circles, shooting at each other, and cursing the day they'd started the chase.

He rolled back over on his belly and sneaked a wary look behind him. All he could see was his horse in the distance, swishing its tail, contentedly nibbling grass. No outguards sneaking up on him this time. No, what was left of the gang was inside.

A window had been opened on the near side. Curtains danced gaily outward. He cocked an ear and could hear her laugh lightly.

• • • •

At noon of the third day they reached Kingman. Thirty-odd miles from Union Pass and the crossover into Nevada. Then California. So far the trip had been free of any threat to the seven passengers or His Majesty, King Philip. Comfortable in his compartment beneath their feet.

Ben ate lunch in the saloon across the street from the only restaurant in town. It was where the driver and shotgun messenger escorted their passengers. Ben could see the girl sitting at a window table. She was talking animatedly to one of the other passengers. He had striking white hair. He was bearded and huge, a belly on him that would have sparked some kind of snide comment from Bert. His latest favorite for big bellies was "He'd need arms six foot long to pull his boots on." He'd said it so often of late it was worn to a nub.

Bert. Dad. My old man. Certainly the oldest 40-year-old in the territories. Possibly in the western world. Product of a tough life. Combination of hardship and equally hard living.

Ben stirred his coffee. He sipped and stared down the bar to the window and the restaurant across the way. And tumbled into a daydream. The old argument: Bert's never-ending campaign to get him to quit. Put his brain to work for a change. "Before it gets all soggy an' useless."

He ignored him with a vengeance. He couldn't desert him. Which was exactly what it would be if he quit. Together they protected each other. Bert by himself would be far more vulnerable. As would he be. Over and above that he *wanted* to be with him. Wanted, needed his companionship. Even though at times he drove him out of his mind.

He felt the bump at the back of his head. It had become larger than the one at the front. Acquired when his horse threw him. Thank you, Bert.

Bert. He could be infuriating. Frustrating. His obstinacy incredible. He could, as if on cue, snap his mind closed. Like a turtle snaps its jaws. He could be petty, childish, prejudiced, perverse. He could make enemies faster than any man he'd ever met. He drank too much. He ate too little and poorly. He abused his body dreadfully. And denied it. He talked too much; he said the wrong thing. He insulted, criticized, and outraged even perfect strangers. He constantly embarrased him. The skin over his ego had all the thickness of a fly's wing. He never stopped carping and caviling. Nothing his son did was right. He did nothing the way it should be done.

He was nosy. He gossiped, he defamed and slandered as readily and as easily as others breathed. He harbored a hundred ridiculous idiosyncracies. Beginning with a horror of doctors. Ending with an ingrained suspicion of any man who spoke with the slightest trace of an accent. He never made a mistake. He lied, deceived, and dutifully ignored the warning voice of his conscience. Ordering it to "mind its own business" whenever it spoke. His only son, his only family he patronized mercilessly.

Bert. He loved him!

Indeed there was only one cloud over their relationship. One threat. The job. If Bert ever discovered that he, Ben, stuck with Wells Fargo out of more than loyalty, out of a deep-set conviction that Bert needed his protection, his father would probably beat him to death.

The journey resumed. Ben followed. He stayed far enough behind to avoid drawing the passengers' attention. After Vollmer-Bolton, this job was downright boring. And becoming more so by the hour. And he missed Bert. When they got to San Francisco he would have to report to James B. Hume. Hume would asked him what had happened back in Las Palomas. He'd ask him about Bert. In spite of his threat to his father, he would try to cover up for him. He could feel his cheeks begin tingling at the mere thought of lying. And lie he must, until he turned pink as cotton candy. Hume would know he was lying, he wouldn't even have to look at him; he'd know.

He'd get all tangled up and wind up on the griddle, frying to a cinder. If his and Bert's positions were reversed, there'd be no problem. With a face as straight as a parson's, Bert could weave the most fanciful tale, embroidering as he went; an explanation-alibi that Ananias himself would have blushed at. He wouldn't get away with it, but he wouldn't back down from it. And wouldn't let anybody push him down. On he'd carry, heaping the pile to the ceiling until Hume and anybody else listening would throw up their hands and order him off the carpet, out of the office.

And when the door closed behind him they would laugh themselves sick.

It was a gift.

• • • •

Bert woke. He jerked up to a sitting position. Then slammed back down. Over he rolled. He parted the grass slowly and studied the house. They were up and about; he could hear muffled voices and the rattle of pans through the open window. The later sound started his juices in his mouth. He had missed supper, it appeared he was going to miss breakfast as well. He got out his gun and checked it. Attacking the house would be insane; he might get one, possibly a couple. But showing himself would be to beg a bullet. And at this close a range, the first one to come his way could easily be fatal.

He would wait until somebody came out. They'd probably ride into town; he hoped somebody would. Still, having already collected the money, it didn't seem likely.

No one showed until around ten o'clock. Cutler and Maria came out together. The others followed. Donald ran ahead to the barn. All went inside. Bert waited. He strained listening; he could hear rummaging. A horse whinneyed. A buckboard appeared. Cutler was at the reins. Maria sat beside him, the others in the bed. They cut across the sideyard to the subsidiary road bypassing the front of the house, heading south toward Lake Valley. He followed a mile behind their dust pillar. They crossed Berenda Creek and drove through Lake Valley. They followed the rail spur to Nutt. And stopped at the railroad station.

He dismounted some distance from them. His stomach rumbled angry protest against his skipping breakfast. He popped his last chaw of Battle Ax into his mouth and watched Cutler approach the ticket window. Maria, Donald, and the other two stood on the platform, looking up the tracks. Apart from a baggage man loading crates and boxes of various sizes onto his cart, they were the only ones on the platform. The train they intended to take would not be showing for awhile, decided Bert. He guessed an hour.

Cutler rejoined the others and passed out tickets. He did not give one to Donald. He spoke to him. Bert was much too far away to catch what either was saying, but Cutler was doing most of the talking. Donald did most of the nodding. Cutler pointed to the buckboard; Donald nodded. Then they left the platform, walking down the wooden steps and across to the street. He watched them start down it. Then he mounted and rode through the backyards of the buildings on the opposite side. He checked his horse into the first stable he came to, then legged it back the way he had come. He approached the ticket window and inquired about the next train.

"Twelve fifty-two," said the man behind the bars in a gravel voice.

"Gimme a ticket."

"To where?"

"Where does it go?"

The man stared, suddenly nonplussed. "First stop is Deming, then Gage, Lordsbury—last stop in New Mexico—Teviston, Arizona, Willcox, Cochise."

"Okay, okay . . ."

"Dragoon, Benson, Pantano, Vail, Wilmot, Tucson."

"Okay!"

"Last stop in Arizona is Yuma. What'll you have?"

"Gimme to Demin'."

"I'll be swoggled! You make me go through the whole blamed schedule . . ."

"I didn't make you nothin', you was just showing off an' you know it. You gonna sell me a ticket to Demin' or not?"

"Two dollars and ten cents."

"TWO! Chrissakes, where's your gun? Your mask? Demin's less than thirty mile from here . . ."

"Twenty-seven, do you want a ticket or not?"

"It's a outrage! I'll have you know I'm a close personal friend o' Leland Stanford, president o' this there tin-cup trolley line!"

"You are? For heaven's sakes, why didn' you say so?"

"I'm sayin; so now!"

"I apologize, that makes all the difference in the world."

"How much now?"

"Two dollars and ten cents, and when you get to Deming, I suggest you send a wire to Mr. Stanford and ask him to get in touch with me, Orlando Higgins Junior, care of Southern Pacific, Nutt, New Mexico. If he okays it, I'll forward you a credit for two dollars and ten cents. Can I have your home address, please?"

"You're 'bout as funny as a death in the family, you know that? Take your damn two bucks!"

"And ten cents."

He shoved two paper dollars across the little counter; he flung the dime angrily at the face grinning out at him. It struck a bar, bounced back, and hit a front tooth. He picked it up and slapped it on the counter.

"Thaaaaaank you . . ."

He snatched up his ticket. He got a ham sandwich that tasted like salted shoe leather cached between two cedar shingles. He washed it down with a shot of Motherwell's Bourbon. The bartender had never heard of Haggerty's

Morning Dew. When he asked, he gave him a look that questioned its existence. After lunch Bert bought a fresh plug of Battle Ax.

He still had nearly half an hour before train time. He took up his post at the far end of the platform. He sat with his legs dangling over the end. His back to the assembling crowd. Some intended to board. Others had come to see them off. Every so often he would sneak a peek up the platform. Cutler, Maria, and the others came back about five minutes before train time. Moments later the faint sound of chuffing could be heard. A single long blast of the whistle signalled approach.

The platform had come alive with activity. Bert peered out from under his hat brim. Cutler and the others boarded the second car behind the tender. He hurried forward. He grabbed the grab iron of the last passenger car just in front of the mail car. Two cars behind the one they had boarded. One foot on the step, he chanced a look down the platform. There stood Donald. As if feeling Bert's eyes on him, he turned. And recognized him.

The train was preparing to pull out. The whistle blasted. Smoke billowed from inside the driving wheels. People called and shouted. Passengers leaned out the windows. Everything happened at once. Donald hauled iron and blazed away at Bert. Cutler shoved his head out the window, as did Maria. Cutler roared.

"Kill him! Kill him!"

Donald tried his best. Slugs nicked the side of the car. One rang off the iron step. Another off the grab iron an inch above Bert's hand. It set the bar ringing. But the boy was shooting too fast. Too wildly.

Down came the traction sand. The locomotive chuffed and chuffed and chuffed. The whistle blasted, the driving wheels spun and caught. Off rolled the string. Cutler roared and shook his fist. Donald slowed his hand and took careful aim. Too careful, too long aiming. Bert fired and hit him dead center of the breastbone. He caved in like he'd been butted, swinging his head back, rolling his eyes upward. Over he toppled, dead.

The train was picking up speed. Bert rushed forward to catch the grab iron he had let go of when he fired back. Too late. He couldn't catch up. The end of the caboose rolled rapidly by and away. Stack smoke settled thinly down upon the gleaming tracks.

The gunplay had frozen the well-wishers and those who had gotten off the train. The stared at Bert. Two men broke the tableau, moving into action. They knelt on either side of Donald. He had dropped his gun. It had fallen down onto the gravel. Bert hurried forward.

"Somebody get the sheriff! Get a move on! This boy's a cold-blooded killer. Wanted in six territories. I've been trackin' him all the way from Tulsa. The Cutler gang. Get the sheriff, I say! Somebody, anybody! MOVE!

The two men kneeling by the body sprang to their feet and ran off in opposite directions.

"Hey, HEY! Tell him Sheriff Brickman's here. Tulsa, Oklahome, Brickman, Tulsa!"

The crowd continued to stand transfixed, gaping at him. He ran up to the ticket window. "Gimme that rolled up flag behind you."

"I can't, it's company property."

Bert growled, jerked open the side door of the booth and snatched up the red flag, menacing the man back with his iron. The ticket seller raised his hands.

"What the hell . . ."

"Just shut up, you'll get it back. Brickman's the name, Sheriff, Tulsa. This is all legal police business."

Away he flew, gun in one hand, flag in the other. Muttering, seething. The occupants of the platform continued to stand rooted and staring. While the train shrank smaller and smaller as it charged the horizon.

Fourteen

Bert opened the horse up. He lowed his head, grit his teeth, and talked to it soothingly. He clutched the signal flag. The train had a full five-minute headstart. But leaving Nutt it would be mountainous going for many miles. Almost to within sight of Deming. The engineer would reduce speed to as little as five miles an hour. With a little luck he would not only catch up, but get ahead of it. A mile or more would be ideal. He should have little trouble stopping the train.

the trail twisted around outcroppings and boulders. It dipped and climbed. He pushed the horse harder; he could feel her beginning to tire already. The rough terrain was murder on her legs. It was mule country, not horse. But she gave it her all.

He came upon a huge ledge resembling a giant anvil lying on its side. He circled it. He reached the crest, hauling up sharply. Fifty feet below he could see the tracks. And something else. Three men were hard at work. Preparing to blow the tracks. Three nefarious types bent on stopping the train, and relieving the passengers and mail car of their valuables.

"Son of a bitch!"

He could see at a glance they were amateurs. One held a bundle of dynamite sticks as fat as a coffeepot. Enough explosives to blow the engine halfway to Gillyman's Creek, two miles up the line. He could see two additional bundles, only slightly smaller. Too much clout, too few participants, he thought. Holding up a train was a ten-man job, calling for speed and thoroughness. This was taking all the aspects of a bumbling botch. The idea was to stop the train. Not reduce it to scrap iron and kindling, and annihilate the crew and half the passengers.

"Boneheads! Stupid clucks! Boss-simple jackasses! The three of 'em oughta be bored for the hollow horn . . ."

He dismounted and drew. "Hey, down there. Drop the firecrackers an' get 'em up!"

One drew lightning fast. Lead sang by Bert's left ear. The sound ringing off the walls of the cut startled their horses. They stood untethered, unhobbled a short way up the line. Bert threw himself down. They had no cover. But this did not prevent them from putting up a fight. He got one squarely in the head. Dropping him where he stood. A second screamed like a snake-spooked girl. And sprawled across the tracks. The survivor wisely dropped his gun. Up went his hands.

"Don' shoot. We din' mean no harm."

"Hell no, just a buncha' good ol' boys out for a lark, right?"

"Don' kill me, please I come from church people . . ."

"They must be proud o' you. Get your horses." Again he fired. Dust kicked at the man's feet. He jumped awkwardly.

"Hey!"

"Get 'em. All three. Bring 'em over. Pile your friends on their saddles and get the hell outta' here. Pronto! I'll give you thirty seconds . . ."

He counted off the seconds. Just for the fun of it. It took the man thirty-four to carry out his instructions.

"Now haul ass outta' here before I change my mind and pot you proper."

"Yes, sir. Sir?"

"What?"

"You with the railroad?"

"President Stanford, that's me."

"No kiddin'?"

Bert ended the conversation with a shot that skinned the edge of the man's hat brim. He swallowed hard and barreled away. He dragged the other horse after him, his companions draped over their saddles. He was out of sight in seconds.

Just in time. The train was coming. Bert could hear it laboring up the grade. He cursed. Given one more minute, he would have been able to blow a track with a single stick of dynamite. He scrambled down the steep incline, setting rocks and gravel rattling down with him. He slid the last few yards on the seat of his pants, clutching the flag. He yelped and swore when a sharp rocked scraped his cheek as he passed over it.

He ran to the railbed and hid the three bundles of dynamite behind convenient rocks. Smoke rose a hundred yards in front of him. The engine came chuffing into view. Straddling the tracks, he waved the flag back and forth. The engineer leaned out of his side of the cab, the fireman out the other. Both saw him, but the train did not slow.

"Stop the damn thing, goat brain! THE BRAKE! THE BRAKE!"

It was impossible for either to hear him, but the brake was pulled. The driving wheels froze, steel against steel singing like a host of banshees in chorus. The sound was earsplitting. On came the rivet-studded behemoth. Bert dropped the red flag. He began backing off. He stopped, looked again, turned and ran, nearly tripping over a tie. He stopped a second time and turned. The engine was slowing. It jolted to a stop.

"What in Sam Hill's goin' on!"

The engineer stared at him bewildered. Bert stepped off the bed to his right, mindful that Cutler and the others were seated on the other side. If they looked out they could not see him now. The trainman and conductor swung down and came hurrying toward him.

"The trestle's down over Gillyman's Creek."

"Who says?" The firemen still in the cab frowned. "How could it be, Gillyman's been dry for six weeks."

"Wasn't a flood. Somebody blew it up. Crew's been workin' on it since sunup. They'll be finished in about ten minutes."

The trainman and conductor came running up. The engineer descended from his perch. He wiped his face with his bandanna.

"Just ten more minutes, that's all. Gallagher, the foreman, sent me to warn all trains. My brother Ted's warnin' em' on the other side."

"Who wrecked the trestle?" asked the trainman.

Bert shrugged. "Could be Injuns. What's the time?"

"East past one," said the conductor. He consulted a watch the size of a baseball.

"Jus' a few more minutes now . . ."

"You already told us," said the conductor. He eyed the engineer who had come up alongside him. "We'll have to make it up on the flat, Bob."

Passenger stuck their heads out windows.

"You boys headin' for Demin'?" he asked. "Mind if I board? My horse is up top." The conductor eyed him skeptically. "Oh, she hasn' et or drunk nothin'. She won't make no mess. She'll just stand in the baggage car smilin' an' swishin' her tail."

"Smiling?"

"Let 'em on, Avery," said the engineer. "He's an employee and he's sure done us a favor."

"Get your horse," said the trainman.

The conductor, outvoted, acquiesced. The trainman turned and was walking back down the train.

"It's okay, folks, just a little delay. We'll be on our way

in a few shakes. Sorry for the holdup. Pull in your heads, there's woodpeckers in these hills."

Nobody laughed, but they pulled in their heads. Bert got his horse up the ramp into the baggage car. He boarded the first car, working the opposite side of the train, out of Cutler's view in the event he looked out. Bert sat down next to an enormous young woman, her tiny rosebud mouth atop a stack of four chins. She wore a frilly, green dress that looked as if it had been wrapped around her and pinned out of sight at the back. she was sweating buckets, fanning herself with a limp lump of hanky.

"Hot day."

She stared at him in a manner that suggested his mastery of the obvious was beyond peer.

"Well it is."

The engineer waited out the time, started up, and away they chuffed. They passed the would-be holdup man and his dead friends. Bert waved. They crossed Gillyman's Creek. Not a soul was in sight. The trestle was old and weather-ravaged, but conspicuously intact, with not a single new board or spike in it.

"Ain't nobody been working at this bridge," said a sour-looking man across the aisle from Bert as they crossed. "Thought you said it was blown up?"

"It was. You shoulda' seen it this mornin'; woulda' made you sick to look at it. Vandalism sure does cost the line a pretty penny."

"Humph."

Bert grinned. He slid into a slouch and tilted his hat down over his face. In seconds he was asleep and snoring. On fanned his overweight companion, her bulbous face ascowl with disapproval.

Fifteen

Darkness settled over the city by the bay. And over the bay settled a fog as thick as a Rocky Mountain rain cloud. It obscured sight of the vessels anchored there. It cloaked the black water. It extinguished the reflections of moon and stars. Through the city the fog crept. Spreading, crawling down the streets. Creeping into alleys. It polished the cobblestones and lampposts. It left in its wake a glistening sheen.

The lamplighters were abroad. Igniting at every other corner a ball of saffron light in its glass housing. Sending a dusty glow down upon the dampened city.

Ben's curiousity over what Maria Stewart's doubloons were intended to purchase became a firm conviction. He had little else to think about over the final three days of the journey. But how and when and with whom would the transaction be made?

Upon arriving in town he was supposed to report to

James B. Hume. But the stage did not get in until long after business hours. The express building offices were closed. He would have to wait until morning. For this he was grateful. He was tired; Hume's questions could wait.

He stood holding his horse across the street from the depot. He squinted through the swirling gray intruder, watching the passengers debark the stage. They looked through the fog as shades stepping off Charon's ferry, having just arrived in Hades. Specters floating lightly afoot, their features indistinguishable through the fog. He counted only five. The two others stayed on board as the driver backed the stage into the shed out of his sight. He continued to wait, watching those who had emerged outside disperse. Presently the street was empty of sound and shadowy movement. Ten minutes passed before a small wagon rolled up. Two hulking shapes came out of the shed. One carried luggage, the other matching small satchels. So the doubloons had been removed from their compartment and placed in satchels.

The three drove away. Ben crossed the street and checked his horse with one of the night men in the shed whom he happened to know. He followed King Philip and his protectors on foot. He followed for six dreary, empty blocks, the wagon emerging at last into a large square. Across the way stood the Palace Hotel, its yellow lights dulled, enfeebled by the fog. He watched them enter, gave them time to register and go up to their rooms. He then crossed and entered the lobby. He got inside just in time to see them step into the elevator.

The hotel was awesomely impressive. It stood eight stories high and reputedly cost its builder, banker William C. Ralston, a million dollars a floor. It boasted a legion of marble statues, colonnades, a fountain big enough to float half a dozen rowboats, silks, damask, furniture of exotic woods, clocks, hardware, and blankets from Ralston's own factories, and flooring from a ranch he had purchased solely for its oak trees.

Its grandeur was lost on Ben. He hurried to the desk, registered, and was given his key. But he did not go upstairs. Instead he walked to the newspaper stand at the end of the lobby and bought a copy of the *San Francisco Examiner*. He no sooner settled in a chair to read it than the elevator doors parted and out came two of the three Mexicans. One carried one of the satchels. They decided to walk to their destination. He followed. As he expected, they headed toward the waterfront. A foghorn voiced its melacholy, montonous note. Seagulls shrilled. Silence returned, broken only by the soft clicking sound of the two men's heels. He stayed a block and more behind them. From the next street over came the rattle of wheels over the cobblestones, the sound fading, fading, losing itself in quiet. There seemed to be no one about until he turned a corner and came upon an elderly lamplighter. The man saluted as he passed. A block beyond Ben began to hear water softly lapping at pilings. Again the foghorn uttered its mournful note. It was answered in kind from far across the bay. As he moved through his unearthly surroundings, the sudden shattering of glass above and behind him startled him. He jerked convulsively.

From what he could see at a distance through the fog, not a word passed between the two men. They turned a corner, and when he followed he saw them stop in front of a large warehouse. The sound of lapping water came from the end of the alley alongside it. They stood reading the sign over the entrance, making certain they had come to the right address. They approached and tried the front door; it was locked. There was no glimmer of light within. They started down the alley, the darkness swallowing them up.

He could barely make out the faded lettering on the sign. Pacific Shipping Company, Inc. 186. He started down the alley, keeping his back against the wall. And stopped almost immediately as a door opened on the right at the end. It flung light outward, revealing a small loading platform with four steps ascending to it. The two went inside. The door closed. The blackness of the pit was restored to the alley. He felt his way along the wall down the alley. Rods of light appeared at the tops and bottoms of double doors. He made his way round the rear corner and stepped up onto a wharf that ran laterally across the back of the building. A freighter lay at anchor some fifteen feet from the wharf. It was shrouded from mast to waterline in darkness, broken only by the light from two small lamps fore and aft. The wooden skeleton of a fire escape loomed darkly. It zig-zagged upward. He climbed. The steps creaked. He ascended on the tips of his toes. And winced at every creak. He reached the roof and crawled out onto it. The shingles smelled stongly of mildew. It revived recollection of his crossing the roof of the hideout in the mountains outside Aztec. But this roof had no chimney.

There was, however, a skylight. More than one. He made his way to the nearest and peered down. Standing amongst tall piles of crates were the two Mexicans, with another man. He was cleanshaven, in shirt sleeves; he wore a celluloid eyeshade. The satchel containing the doubloons sat on a table within easy reach of the visitors. The three stood talking animatedly. Ben gripped the edge of the skylight frame. He tried to lift it so that he might hear, but it was locked from inside.

He lay prone and watched. The man directed the others' attention to three large water-tank wagons standing side by side. They were made of oak; they looked to be brand-new. Their metal staves and the wheel hubs gleamed brightly. The man was looking about. Searching. He found a tin cup; he filled it with water from a spigot. And offered it to one of the men. He drank. Then the warehouseman, G. Roswell, whoever, got a crow-bar out and set about opening a long crate. Ben squinted. He was able to make out two words stenciled on the lid: Springfield, Massachusetts.

He could not hear the men talking. But the squealing of the nails as they were loosened penetrated the glass.

Sixty thousand dollars in gold for rifles for Howling Wolf's Mimbres army. The wagons were obviously specially built to work practically, dispensing water from their spigots. Containing a limited supply purely for show. The space inside the tanks was to be filled with rifles and ammunition.

The crate was opened: the man ripped through the oiled

paper covering. He lifted out a shiny new carbine: an army-issue Springfield. Probably brought up the coast from Mexico by the freighter anchored behind the warehouse. In the hands of the Apaches, even the boys, such weapons could conceivably restore the tribe's control over southern New Mexico. And eastern Arizona.

He watched as the man attached a twenty-inch bayonet to the muzzle. His visitors nodded approvingly. He then opened a box of cartridges. The Mexicans lifted handfuls of them and let them fall.

The man got out a bottle and three glasses. And poured for a toast.

"To success," said Ben. "To the death of white-eyes."

They drank. The satchel was then opened. The man reached into it and let a handful of doubloon sift through his fingers. As the Mexican had with the cartridges. The satchel was then emptied onto the barrelhead. The doubloons were carefully counted back into the satchel. The counting was completed. The man removed the lid from the barrel. He placed the satchel inside and nailed the lid down. Then he rolled the barrel to the cage. He unlocked the door and placed it inside.

A second round of drinks was enjoyed by all. This signalled the end of the meeting. The two Mexicans left by the platform door as they had entered. Ben lingered at the skylight. He watched the man return after he had locked the door. He opened the cage, loosened the barrel lid, got out a single doubloon, kissed it ardently, and pocketed it.

A question raised itself in Ben's weary mind. Others quickly followed it. When would the second satchel be brought and the weapons loaded? When would the wagons leave? Tomorrow night? Or during the day? There was no reason he could think of why they shouldn't leave during the day. Three water-tank wagons in the streets certainly wouldn't arouse any suspicion. But loading them was another matter. Perhaps the man with the celluloid eyeshade was the only warehouse employee involved in the transaction. Perhaps whoever owned or managed the place knew nothing whatsoever about the shipment. Or the doubloons.

If this was the case, the Mexicans would probably not return with the second and final payment until the following night. Show up, pay, and leave with their purchase.

And yet it would be foolish to take chances. As soon as he was finished with Hume—rather, as soon as Hume was finished with him—he would come back.

Sixteen

CAPTURED BY SAVAGES STOP I ESCAPED STOP FATHER STILL PRISONER STOP HAVE FOOLPROOF ESCAPE PLAN BUT NEED MONEY TO PURCHASE HORSE GEAR WEAPONS STOLEN BY CAPTOR STOP HURRY MATTER LIFE AND DEATH

BS

Ben read the telegram pushed across the desk by James B. Hume and looked up at his chief. Hume tilted his handsome head to one side, turning one-quarter profile, closing one eye and fixing the other fiercely upon Ben's own. As if in anticipation that the first words out of his mouth would be a lie and that he was being fairly forewarned not to utter them.

"Well?" asked Hume.

"Well what?"

"Are you twins?"

"I don't understand."

"Oh no, it's *I* who don't understand. Correct me if I'm wrong. You set out from Hatch on the morning of the twenty-eighth after I sent you the money you wired me for. You then left by train for Tucson. Later the same day I get this wire from Las Palomas. Would you kindly explain how you could be on a train riding to Tucson and in Las Palomas at the same time? On second thought, you needn't bother. Where is he?"

"You mean Bert?"

"Ben..." Hume was beginning to redden. His eye aimed at Ben grew fiercer.

"All right, all right... Maybe he did try to dupe you into..."

"He didn't dupe anybody. He's incapable of duping. I sent him money *after* I sent you yours. Only because he asked for it. I'm not stupid; I knew he was playing games. I couldn't be bothered figuring out why. I ask you again, where is he?"

"Someplace in or around Las Palomas."

"That's pretty vague. You're supposed to be a team; each of you's supposed to know where the other is at all times. He's off on his own hook chasing Cutler, isn't he? Flagrantly disobeying orders. As usual."

"He was captured by Apaches."

"I don't care if cannibals got him!" Down came Hume's fist, pounding the desk. "I stick my neck out three feet for him! I protect him at the risk of my job, and this is the thanks I get!"

"He's not chasing Cutler."

"Don't lie to me, Ben."

"He can't be. They were both captured by the Mimbres. Bert got away. Cutler tried to and was killed."

"You know that for a fact?"

"I..."

"Or is that what your father told you?"

"Would you let me explain? Let me try?"

"One or the other, Ben. Preferably the first."

Ben told all. Then, with scarcely pause to breathe, he moved onto Tucson: the three passengers, the doubloons, the goings-on at the Pacific Shipping Company warehouse.

"Bert's tailing the woman, Maria Stewart."

"Why? Who asked him to?"

"I guess I'm not making myself clear. The guns are earmarked for the Mimbres. Once they're into their hands, there'll be a bloodbath the likes of which hasn't been seen in that neck of the woods since the old days. Innocent white people butchered by the hundreds. The Army'll be helpless to save them . . ."

"I understand that. There's something you should understand, it's not the company's business."

"IT'S EVERYBODY'S BUSINESS!"

"Don't shout . . ."

"Don't make me!"

Hume clamped his mouth shut, deliberately cutting off his response. He turned full face forward. The fire had gone out of his eyes, displaced by their usual mildness.

"Ben, I shouldn't need to remind you that I have to answer to Superintendant Valentine and Mr. Tevis himself. What do you suppose they'd say if I told them one of our detectives was up to his ears in tracking down some renegade Mexican woman bent on arming the Indians? What do you think they'd tell me to do with Bert?"

"Fire him."

"Exactly."

"Fire the best detective you've got."

"The best, no argument. Although if you ever tell him I said so, I'll break your neck. But fire him. Whether he's willing to recognize it or not, we operate under a strict set of rules. We have to. The first rule is that when an order comes down from this office to a man in the field, *that order is to be obeyed*!"

"Please listen. Those weapons will be leaving to go back east to the Burro Mountains. To somewhere in the vicinity sometime tomorrow. I want your permission to follow them. I guarantee they'll lead me straight to her, and through her to Bert. The minute we hook up we'll start back here. I give you my word on it."

Hume said nothing. Instead, he pulled open a drawer and lay a file on the desk. Ben opened it. It contained material on a case involving the planned wreck of a Central Pacific train. The thieves had made off with $100,000 in gold bars after killing two mailmen. Hume tapped the open folder.

"This is already three days cold, thanks to his lollygagging. This is where you'll be going, Sacramento. Not Las Palomas or Tucson or anywhere else."

"Have it your way." Ben closed the folder and stood up. "I quit. You'll have my written resignation within the hour."

"Now just a minute, Ben . . ."

"I said I quit. I'm leaving, have a pleasant day."

"Come back here, you young pup!" Ben stopped with his hand on the doorknob. "You're as ornery as your old man."

"Mr. Hume . . ."

"Shut up, can't you see I'm thinking?"

Ben moved to the window. He gazed out over the bay. The mist of morning had displaced the fog of the night before, and was now itself lifting. The sun silvered the blue water. It looked so cool, so refreshing, he was tempted to raise the window and dive in. Boats eased slowly about. Gulls shrilled.

"You think you can find him?"

"We'll be looking for each other. He knows I'm coming back."

"It's all so wild. Completely harebrained . . ."

"He's got her within reach. The guns will be going to her. I'll be following . . ."

"I could be tossed into the bay so fast . . ."

Hume glanced at the door, making certain it was closed. Even so, he lowered his voice.

"Lock the door." Ben complied. "Fired out of my chair. You don't know Mr. Tevis, he's like a bull terrier. He gets his teeth into whatever and never lets go. You walk out that door and in ten minutes, maybe sooner, he'll be in here firing questions at me about the two of you. What am I supposed to do for answers? Eh? By the Lord Harry, I'd have to be the biggest fool in Christendom to let you go running back there . . ."

"Then you agree."

"I DIDN'T SAY THAT! I . . . didn't . . ."

"We'll be back here in a week. Both of us." Ben winced and nearly bit the tip of his tongue. Why gild the lily of cooperation? Why hand the man a whip he might later have cause to thrash him with?

"The sooner the better." Hume sighed. "I'll have to assign Warburton Harpending Junior and Ed Eck to the Sacramento thing." He got out a La Flor de Portuondo, Chico cigar; he clipped off the tip with his watch chain clipper and lit up. Ben watched as he built a smoke screen between them. The meeting was over.

"I must get back to that warehouse . . ."

"You do that. One last thing. I've said it before, I'll keep saying it till it sinks in. This organization is not in the business of subsidizing private feuds. And I'll believe Cutler's dead the day you bring me his newspaper obituary. *And* a photograph of him in his coffin. You might tell that to Egbert."

"I will, Mr. Hume, and thank you."

"Get out of here before I change my mind. And for pity's sakes, keep in touch. It's the least you can do. I'm sitting back here in the lion's cage suspended over his jaws." He nodded toward the wall separating his office from Tevis's.

Ben grinned and nodded. Hume dismissed him with a flip of his hand.

• • • •

He could not get to the fire escape in the rear without drawing attention to himself. He hesitated to attempt it, not wishing to be button-holed by one or another employee. He would wait until the place closed at six o'clock.

It was still light out when the workday ended and everyone left. He gave it an additional fifteen minutes, then made his way down the alley and up onto the roof. The fog was already beginning to accumulate over the water. Within the hour, it would launch its nightly invasion of the city. Below, through the skylight, he could see the crates and boxes standing as before. And the three wagons. The crates containing the carbines were still stacked in the cage. The barrel in which the man had placed the satchelful of doubloons had not been moved.

He waited nearly three hours for darkness. He listened to the bickering of seagulls and the tooting and whistling of traffic about the bay. As he watched the birds soar effortlessly over the tranquil water the fog closed in in earnest, erasing sight of them.

It was foggy but not yet completely dark when a voice startled him. He had been lying prone at the skylight, lost in recollection of the events of the previous two weeks. He glanced down the roof toward the rear. The masts of the freighter anchored near the wharf rose eerily, high above the roof. A deckhand had climbed to the crow's nest. Ben could barely distinguish his face. It was beady eyed, belligerent looking. He scowled questioningly.

"What in Tophet you doing there?"

"Inspecting the skylights. What does it look like? I'm with the Eccols Skylight Company, office in all major cities. The sealing on this one needs replacing. It's rotted away to nothing."

"Bilge water! Who are you? What do you want?"

"I just told you."

"You're a liar."

"Then I'm a liar. Try minding your own business, sailor boy."

"We'll see about that. Clinton! Hey, Clinton, come up here. Wanta' show you something. CLINTON! Oh, for cryin' out loud . . ."

He started down. The instant his head vanished form sight, Ben scrambled for the front of the building. The roof was tilted just enough toward the back to let rain run off. There was only the one fire escape, but he found three other skylights. The first was locked, the second one he got lucky. He got it open, threw a leg over the edge and pulled the top down with one hand, feeling for footing below as he did so. A crosspiece connected the lower portions of two overhead supporting beams. He slipped one leg over the piece and, still gripping the skylight catch while bracing himself with his free hand, managed to pull the skylight closed. At the same time, he slipped his other leg over the crosspiece. Down he fell, hanging upside down by his legs.

Down fell his wallet, slapping the floor lightly some forty feet below.

"Damn!"

The blood began rushing to his head. He looked straight down into darkness that seemed to reach all the way to Hell. Then, straining his eyes, he craned his neck and glanced about the ceiling. The three other skylights, like the one he was under, resembled double slabs of slate. Each was fitted below with dual crosspieces like the one from which he hung. He could see no possible way of getting to the nearest wall. There was nothing other than his perch to hang onto. He fleetingly thought of skinning the cat and then dropping feet first. But he was much too high up. He'd break both legs and his neck.

He waited, upside down like a bat. He cocked an ear, straining to hear what was going on outside. Muffled shouting. Footsteps ran up the alley. Then all was silent. He could hear both doors tried in turn. He wondered how long he could hang and gave himself ten more minutes.

He fished out his watch. He held it two inches from him. And still could barely make out the hands. At the six-minute mark, his head began poundingly relentlessly. Black spots swam into his vision of the skylight less than four feet above. Smearing it. The spots danced, vanished, reappeared. At seven minutes he heard loud talking outside. Evidently the search was over.

At eight minutes he gave up. He began to swing like a trapeze artist; he swung high enough to get hold of the inner edge of the skylight. But let it go. Again he swung, hands outstretched. They struck the glass; they pushed it open. He clutched the edge and pulled upward. His legs, then his feet abandoned his perch.

He climbed through and dropped onto the roof. His heart pounded furiously. The ordeal had exhausted him. He lay listening; he could hear nothing other than the water lapping the pilings. He glanced at the crow's nest. The fog swirled around it eerily. No sign of his antagonist. He closed the skylight and moved stealthly to the rear. He peered over the edge at the deck below. No one was about.

He climbed down the fire escape and went around the corner into the alley. Like the men searching for him, he too tried the door entering on the loading platform. As he expected, it was locked. He circled the building around front and moved down the opposite side. There were no windows but under the wharf he found a space; it was crammed with equipment. He struck a match. He let it flare and burn only an instant. Just long enough to get a glimpse. Under the wharf were lamps, coiled hawsers, oars, rope, a makeshift ladder, even a rusty anchor. He got out a rope fifty to sixty feet long and began tying knots in it about 20 inches apart.

He returned to the roof. He tied one end of the rope to his perch under the skylight and started down hand over hand. He was 21 knots down and counting when the rope snapped, dropping him the last few feet.

He landed unhurt. He glanced upward at the skylight, then struck a match and looked about for his wallet. He found it, coiled the rope, went to the loading platform door to let himself out. His hand on the upper bolt, he paused.

He could let himself out easily. But there would be no way he could relock the door behind him. When the warehouse man arrived and went to open it to let in his two business partners and found it unlocked . . .

He was considering this when he heard the front door rattle. He blew out his fifth match. Someone came in. More than one person. Four, possible five. He could hear a foreign language. Chinese? It sounded like it. Then English and broken English. He began feeling his way through the darkness. Bumping into boxes, barking his shins, biting his lip to keep from yelling in pain. He got down behind a large crate. Just in time. Around the corner of the crate he saw a lamp being lit. And the man from the night before come it. With him were four Chinese in black pillbox caps, pajamas, and slippers. They wore their hair in long queues. The man led them to the cage containing the carbines. He unlocked it and got out his doubloon barrel, rolling it to one side.

He got a screwdriver and opened all three tank wagon ends. From behind his crate Ben could see straight into the middle wagon. About six inches up from the bottom a second, false bottom had been installed. Under it lay a small metal tank. A length of hose connected it to the exterior spigot.

The four Chinese talked in low tones. All five were obviously waiting for Mexicans. Ben, too, waited. A knock presently sounded at the platform door. The man opened it for them and in they trouped. There were three this time. They carried their luggage and matching satchel.

The second payment of doubloons. The satchel was set on top of the barrel. The Chinese went to work. In seconds the air was filled with the squealing of nails being loosened and crates thumping the floor. The carbines were removed from their crates and piled inside the water tanks. Boxes of cartridges were also packed. Ben whistled silently in wonderment; he roughly estimated that at least a thousand carbines were loaded. Each was equipped with a bayonet. And he counted nearly a hundred boxes of cartridges. The workers were fast, efficient, and tireless. It took less than half an hour to complete the transfer. the warehouse man paid them and they left.

He went out to lock the door after them. The moment he was out of sight, his three visitors began talking in Spanish. Ben could not understand a word, so rapidly did they talk. He didn't need to. Their expressions said that the warehouse man was in for trouble.

He came back all smiles. He got out a bottle and they

toasted the occasion. While his guests continued drinking, he restored the three tank ends.

"When are you leaving?" he asked.

"Right away," said one of the men.

"Your horses are across the street. A Mr. Whitelaw is expecting you. He's already been paid . . ."

His eyes drifted to the second satchel. One of them caught his hint and opened it for his inspection. He started at the sight of the contents. Ben snickered. He should be accustomed to the sight by now. And make some small effort to conceal his avarice. Ben watched as he picked up two handfuls of doubloons and let them sift slowly through his fingers. He licked his lips as he did so. Ben's eyes were still on him when a soft, whirring sound intruded upon the clinking of the coins.

The man who had come in with the Mexicans was standing ten feet from the warehouse man's back. He had thrown a knife. It struck the greedy one squarely between the shoulder blades. He grunted, put on a look of astonishment, and caved in.

The barrel was opened, the first satchel removed. Its contents were checked. Then the lifeless man's body was unceremoniously dumped into the barrel and the top nailed in place.

Ben could feel no sympathy for him. He had died wealthy but would be buried without his ill-gotten gold. He watched the two big men, whom he had come to take for granted were brothers, go out the front way. They returned shortly bringing three teams. They backed the horses into the shafts and hitched them. One of the men then pocketed the unfortunate warehouse man's screwdriver.

They finished their host's bottle before leaving. The one who had killed him sat on the barrel containing his corpse. He laughed, joked, enjoyed himself relaxing. And complimented the quality of the liquor in English.

When they were finished drinking, they loaded their suitcases and the two satchels and drove out the front way. They took the lamp with them, plunging the interior into darkness. Ben heard the door close. It was left unlocked.

He let them go without following. There was no need; he knew where they were going. He also knew that he could travel four times as fast and would have no difficulty catching up. Possibly as soon as Westley or Crows Landing on the way to Tulare Lake. Below the lake lay Bakersfield. South of Bakersfield the route turned directly eastward.

How ironic, he thought. To fetch the doubloons eleven-hundred-odd miles just to display. Close the deal, murder the supplier, retrieve the gold, and start back. King Philip certainly was a well-travelled man.

He yawned and stretched. There wasn't much time between trips for rest and relaxation, he noted. Still, he would be in better shape for the return than any of them. He looked forward to a good night's sleep and a hearty breakfast in the morning.

He made a mental note to make two small but very important purchases before leaving town tomorrow.

Seventeen

Ben stopped by the office after breakfast. He wanted to bring James Hume up to date. In small measure repay him for his cooperation. The last time he'd seen him, Hume had been distressed over the situation. A bad night's sleep had since given him to the day in woeful shape. Ben was surprised. Hume was not the nervous sort by nature. He had a temper, he could get upset, he was conscientious and therefore a worrier. A bachelor, he had no one to worry to but he generally kept a firm grasp on his emotions.

Not this morning. Watching and listening to him, Ben felt sorry for the man. And for himself and Bert. In creeping out on a limb for them Hume was flirting with disaster. If Tevis were to get wind of it . . .

"He'd come down on me like a brick wall!"

"He won't know a thing about it. Unless you tell him."

"You don't know him. He has ways. Keep your voice down; he could be listening at the wall. Better yet, get out of here. Use the back stairs. If you spot him in the hallway, duck out of sight."

Ben stifled a chuckle. He left. He went directly to Julius Bandmann's shop next door to his manufacturing plant on Boyle Street. In 1866 Bandmann began making the first dynamite ever manufactured in the United States. He was still at it. Ben signed the necessary authorization paper in duplicate. This permitted him to purchase six sticks of dynamite and 30 feet of Bickford safety fuse. Flexible enough to wind on a spool and consisting of a core powder surrounded by twisted strands of jute. This was wrapped with a layer of twine and then with a second outside wrapping of waterproof tape. Ben knew from experience that the fuse burned at a reliably uniform rate and seldom failed. Even if it did, it tended to fizzle out rather than burn too fast and set off a premature explosion.

From Bandmann's he went down the street and around the corner to Warrengard's Specialty Shop. There he bought a three-dollar spyglass with black-morocco-covered body, burnished-brass draw tubes, achromatic lenses and a magnifying power of ten diameters.

It was ten o'clock in the morning when he left San Francisco. He planned to retrace the stage route. It would bring him to Haywards and Westley beyond.

• • • •

Cutler, Maria, and the other two got off the train in Maricopa. Every time the train stopped before arriving there, Bert would snap awake. He would stretch and lean across his overweight fellow passenger to look out the window. She had offered to swap seats with him even before they crossed over into Arizona. Each time she repeated her offer he declined politely. "I wouldn' wanna' put you out." His good manners notwithstanding, hostilities were only avoided when she got off at Willcox.

They did not reach Maricopa until late afternoon. The day was dawdled away stopping at every town, hamlet, and settlement boasting more than two buildings along the way. Bert watched Cutler and the others gather on the station platform. Then he ran back through the cars and got off the last one on the track side of the string. He got the attention of the trainman and two minutes later his horse was led down the ramp. He did not come around the end of the train to claim it until the engine hooted and prepared to pull out. When he did, he saw to his dismay that Cutler and his party had left.

But there had not been time enough for them to get far. He spotted them in front of the local stable. Hiring a buckboard. They bought food for themselves before leaving town.

He followed a safe half-mile behind their dust. He flirted with the idea of following until nightfall, then taking them when they stopped for the night. But thought better of it. Maria's appearance and her newly forged alliance with Cutler pricked his curiosity. What, he wondered, were they up to? He would find out before he took care of Cutler. Could they be running off to get married? If that were so, why bring along the others? Second thought painted the first as absurd. Marriage to the greasy-haired snake had to be the furthest thing from her mind. Their partnership was strictly business.

What business?

He would follow and find out before he made his play. They headed north. He guessed they would stop for the night in Tempe on the far side of the Gila River. But they did not. They drove on through Tempe and crossed the Salt River. And camped in the open on the north bank.

The country was desolate, burning hot by day, bitter cold by night. The stars pulsed in their multitudes in the cobalt sky. The moon was in its first quarter, a slice of melon poised on end. Bert tied his mount to a clump of sagebrush. He crawled forward on his belly to within 30 feet of their fire. He could smell coffee and bacon. His last meal had been in Arizola, two stops before Maricopa. He had eaten well, two thick roast beef sandwiches washed down with a pint of Clubman Beer. He figured it could be some time till his next meal, and had gorged himself accordingly.

The breeze came to life. It snatched at the fire, tearing, nearly smothering it. And passing on. The flame came back to life. Cutler and Maria sat side by side. He scowled into the fire. It lent him the likeness of a one-eyed demon. She was talking.

"Brooding about it won't bring him back."

"Damn engineer wouldn' even stop the train. Can you beat that?"

"You could have stopped it yourself. All you had to do was pull the emergency cord."

"It all happened so fast."

"He was very young . . ."

"Just turned seventeen. Younges' of all. My baby brother. Now he's dead, gunned down by that Wells Fargo bastard!"

"Must you continually swear?"

"It's what he is, a bastard! Baby killer. May he rot in hell. If I ever run into him again I'll stomp him to death! No, first I'll torture him. Make him scream for mercy. I'll put his skin off inch by inch."

"Sure," said Bert. And bit off a chaw of Battle Ax.

He mulled over Cutler's revelation. And didn't know whether to be surprised or elated. All the time he'd been with them, Cutler and Donald had never even hinted they were related. They did call each other by their first names, but all of them called Cutler by his.

His younger brother. There was no family resemblance he could see, but that didn't mean anything. Other than their eyes, there was little between himself and Ben.

Cutler's kid brother. Harmonica and all. dead, and he'd killed him. Was that justice or what? Ariel would be dancing in heaven to hear it!

No. She didn't believe in an eye for an eye. She had too much breeding, too much class. It showed in their relationship. She'd never let him feel his inferiority to her. Whenever he brought up the differences in their backgrounds she'd snap him quiet. What a woman. What a heart . . .

"It does pay back some, darlin'. Not much but a little.

But don' worry, I'll finish the job. I'll get us payment in full!''

No to that, too. Killing Cutler could never be full compensation for what he'd done. Every inch of him wasn't worth one of her eyelashes. The devil and the angel. The scum of the earth and the flower of womanhood. Nevertheless, he had to die. Be killed. Bert wondered: *Was* vengeance as sweet as everybody claimed? He'd find out, and soon.

''Some day I'm goin' back to Nutt an' find out where they buried Donald. I'll dig him up and give him a proper funeral. Bes' money can buy. Glass window hearse, two coal black high-steppers, heaps an' heaps o' flowers, a honest-to-God preacher. If ever a soul deserved the best . . .''

He sniffed and wiped his nose with the back of his hand. Bert blinked. A tear had emerged from his working eye. It glistened down his cheek.

''Hey, Rance,'' said one of the others, ''how's about I go into town an' get us a bottle?''

''Forget it.''

''But it's cold, I need a little fire in my gut.''

''I'll go with you,'' said the other man.

''You stay put, I'll go.''

Bert watched Cutler get to his feet and dust off his seat.

''I'd rather you didn't,'' said Maria.

''Shut up, woman,'' said Bert. He started snaking backwards.

''I won't be long. Tranquillity's only about four miles west. I'll be back b'fore you miss me.''

Bert had stopped to catch his last few words. He caught Tranquillity and turning, hurried away to where he had tied his roan. He found her nibbling on a clump of grass.

''Let's go, little girl. You an' me are 'bout to make hist'ry.''

He bent to loosen the reins from the bush, but she had pulled them so tightly he couldn't work them loose. Didn't have the fingernails to. He swore softly as the sound of thumping hooves leaving their camp reached his ears. Then he smiled. Why get all upset? He knew where he was heading. He finally had to stick his face in the sagebrush and loosen the tie with his teeth.

He headed west in the direction graciously supplied him by Cutler. Within minutes, a thin scattering of lights could be seen. Transquillity was tiny and, when he followed Cutler into it, anything but tranquil. The lone saloon exploded with noise and merriment. He pulled up, then eased into the shadows. He watched Cutler dismount in front of the saloon. Before he went in, he undid his shirt. Bert watched him run his hand around his middle. Checking his Wells Fargo loot, he thought.

He wondered what Cutler had in mind. Did he know somebody inside? Somebody he could trust to hold his belt full of goodies while he finished whatever it was Maria had hired him for? Or to hold the money while he ran off to Mexico with his two friends, chased about the mountains, lost them, and came back to collect?

He wouldn't put it past him to do the later. But he wasn't about to show himself inside the saloon just to confirm it. No, he'd let him drink his fill, buy his bottle, and come back out.

He could take him right there: dead-center Tranquillity. Or let him start back and stop him on the way. He'd blow a rivet when he recognized him. He'd go wild. He could just picture his eye . . .

He dismounted and led the roan up to the hitch rack directly opposite the saloon. No sooner did he flip the reins over than an explosion hammered his eardrums. So loud, for a second he feared for his skull. The door in front of him blew open. Smoke poured out. Men boiled out, their faces covered by bandannas. They were greeted by gunfire coming from the batwing doors opposite. Bert ducked. In two seconds, he found himself in the middle of the battlefield. Shots whistled over his head and zinged by in both directions. Slugs dug into the hitch rack. Slammed into the ground. A shot blew through his hat. Firing, yelling, smoke and wild activity were all around him. He was dead! He knew it! He might just as well be down a well. With a Gatling gun pointed straight down and chattering.

He scrunched lower; he swore. He trembled, fear sweat bursting from his pores. An outlaw grabbed him from behind. He jerked him to his feet. Held him by a handful of shirt back. Jammed his gun against his spine.

"What the hell . . ."

"Shut up, pilgrim. If they don't hit you, I will!"

The fire coming from the saloon increased in volume as the good guys' numbers swelled. The gang backed off into the side alley. A rosy-cheeked kid was holding their horses. Bert protested loudly. He was ignored and hauled up onto a big-rumped stallion. Seconds later he was riding away like the winter wind. Hanging onto the midriff of the man in the saddle.

"Be smart," said the rider alongside them. "Be a good shield for Alton's backside and we'll turn you loose when we get clear. Iff'n' you don't . . ."

"All right, all right. You guys are nuts, you'll never get away . . ."

"Already have. With close to four hunnerd bucks!"

Bert threw a look behind them. A posse was assembling. But by the time they got started better than half a mile stretched between.

"PICK IT UP BOYS!" said the man in the lead. "Another mile we'll be roses . . ."

They would be, reflected Bert disgustedly. Of all the freaky things to happen. Nauseating! Humiliating!

All had pulled down their bandannas. There were six. Seven counting the horse minder. They rode in a tight bunch, hard and fast. And faster. Bert locked his hand over his wrist to keep from falling. They had swept into a sharp curve. Through it and back onto the straightaway. The road twisted like a sidewinder. Once more he looked back. No sign of the posse. But the outlaws held their pace. Not one slowed even the slightest.

Ahead a huge outcropping loomed. Bert gasped. It appeared to be sitting in the middle of the road. It was not. But was close enough on the left to reach out and touch as they passed it. Around it, instead of straightening, the curve bent even more sharply. As he realized it and tightened his hold, the man he was hanging onto barked savagely.

"You're squeezin' the breath outta' me, son of a bitch! LEGGO!"

Down came his fist hammering Bert's grip. Forcing him to let go. Like invisible hands, centrifugal force jerked him sharply right. Clear of the horse. Soaring. Landing hard in a patch of short grass.

"OWWWWWWWW!"

Pain shot up his cheek to the base of his spine. He righted himself. He grimaced and rubbed his butt.

"Mangy bastard . . ."

He could no longer see them. Only their dust filling the curve. And the fading sound of their horses. Silence reigned. Then the pounding resumed, coming from behind him. He staggered to his feet. Up they came, two riders pulled free of the pack and headed straight for him. He jumped clear. He got to his feet a second time, cursing, straightening, shutting up. A gun was leveled at his belly, two feet from it.

"One down, seven to go," said the man covering him.

"What the hell you talking about!"

"You heard the man," said his companion. "Let's go."

"Are you nuts? I'm not one of 'em. I got caught in the middle back there. They grabbed me for a shield. Didn' you see?"

"Just shut up and move," said the other grimly. "Where's your horse?"

"Back at the rack in front o' the bank. Likely horsemeat now, thanks to you an' them . . ."

"He don't have no bandanna," said the man covering him. He holstered his iron.

"He threw it away."

"I did not! You're crazy!"

The rest of the posse was long out of sight. Bert continued protesting his innocence, cursing his captors' stupidity with all the vehemence he could muster. To no avail; they had suddenly been stricken deaf.

• • • •

Marshal Ira Alsop looked a little like the late, lamented E. Floyd Gilhuly, noted Bert; until he opened his mouth. His drawl was so thick it barely made it past his store teeth. A half-hour after the two deputies brought him in, Alsop and the rest of the posse had returned empty-handed. Miraculously, Bert's horse had emerged from the fray unscathed. Nobody had been killed or even hurt in the brief exchange, as far as he could see. A small portion of luck had come his way with Alsop's return. He recognized him and confirmed his assertion that he had been an innocent bystander.

"I got to go, Marshal, I got business."

"Business? In Tranquillity? In the middle of the night?"

Bert explained in brief about Cutler. "Last I saw of him, he went into the saloon. By now he's got to be long gone."

"So what's your hurry then?"

"I know where he's headin'."

"Then y'all 'll know wheah he'll be right?"

"Them that's waitin' on him could move on."

"Y'all 'll pick up the trail. Besides, they won't be movin' till sunrise. I only need you for a few minutes."

"A few minutes is too damn long, I'm tellin' you! Can'tcha get it through your head? He's already had a good half-hour, closer to an hour. That's wide country out there . . ."

"Take it easy, take it easy, ya'all'll bust a blood vessel. Do you always get so hot so quick? Relax, ah just want y'all to go through the dodger pile. They all had on bandannas, but y'all have already said they pulled 'em off when they headed out. Y'all musta' seen at least some o' their faces."

"I didn't see nothin'!"

His cheeks were already crimson with anger and frustration threatened to purple. Me and my big mouth, he reflected.

"Just need a few minutes o' your time."

Bert glowered but said nothing. Alsop set a two-foot-high stack of wanted posters in front of him. Bert groaned.

"I don' believe this . . ."

"The quicker y'all get to it, the quicker you'll be outta' heah."

"All right, all right."

He whipped away the first, the second, the third, and jolted upright at the sight of the fourth.

"IT'S HIM!"

"Who?"

"Cutler, the one I'm after."

Alsop read "Rance Cutlah. My, that's a fine ol' southern name. Wanted for murder of Wells Fargo agent E.F. Gilhuly in Fruitland, New Mexico. Wells Fargo and Company will pay one hundred dollars rewahd foh arrest and conviction of Cutlah. Any infohmation regahding accused should be fohwahded to . . ."

"All right, all right! He's here in town, he was." Bert shot to his feet. "I gotta go, I gotta catch up . . ."

"Sit down. Y'all can go as soon as you finish this pile. And theah's a smallah one . . ."

"WHAT!"

"Ah don't care about this whatevah-his-name is . . ."

"Cutler. Chrissakes, can't you read?"

"He's no concern o' ouahs at the moment. What I want from y'all . . ."

The man's infuriating calmness, his slowness, his obstinacy, his utter refusal to listen to reason combined in a great weight of fury. It bent and broke the last cable anchoring Bert's patience. He went wild. He let fly. He smashed the marshal full in the jaw, knocking him flat and cold.

"Jesus . . ."

He cast about. He spotted the key ring. He dragged Alsop back to the cells and locked him up. Then grabbed a Winchester form the rack. He looked for shells and found half a box in the second drawer of the desk. He started for the door. His hand was around the knob when it opened.

There stood two deputies. One was one of the men who had brought him back to town.

"What's goin' on?" he asked. The other man came in. He moved past Bert. "Where's Marshal Alsop?"

"He had to go out."

"What are you doin' with that rifle? Did he say you could borrow it?"

"Course."

The deputy stared. His face darkened with doubt.

"Hey, Willis, come back here," said his partner from inside.

Bert lunged forward. But the deputy was too quick. He shoved his chest in front of him.

"Hold your horses . . ."

Bert sighed at the clinking of the cell door being unlocked. The marshal came out rubbing his jaw. He tested it for fracture. And scowled fiercely.

"Lock him up."

Eighteen

Ben followed them east of Kingman. Up to now the three of them had stuck to the stage route. He had caught up with them just north of Bakersfield. He had carelessly gotten too close coming through Union Pass and had had to cut off the road. He had galloped full tilt for nearly a mile, just so they wouldn't suspect he was following. They had stopped in Bakersfield earlier for nearly the entire afternoon, loading up on food and liquor. In such quantity it appeared they were planning no future stops ahead.

West of Kingman, about ten miles from town, Ben spotted what he assumed to be a Mohave smoke signal. It had turned out to be a private conversation. Having nothing whatsoever to do with the caravan. Tank wagons had to be of little interest to Indians. Or to any outlaws who might notice them.

The heat did not seem to bother the Mexicans. Nor did the nights' bitter cold. They camped and slept around their fire. Before retiring they passed around their bottle. Occasionally they got out one of the satchels and played some kind of card game. Using the doubloons as chips. After every game, however, great care was taken to count the coins before they were put back in their satchel.

The lodes around Kingman had yielded considerable quantities of gold of their own in the past. The town was built on gently sloping land between Hualpai, Cerbant, and Black Mountains. Under the withering summer heat, the plant life bore evidence of its struggle to survive. The area was extremely arid. The cacti dropped. Branches were reduced to thorns and stubs. Leaves were varnished or dropped altogether. The sky glowed with carmines, chrome yellows, and the yellow of the palo verde washed across the desert to the horizon, where sky, mountains, and cacti dissolved into a purple haze. Creatures crept into the shade of the mesquite. Only the lizard braved the sun's glare. And the three protectors of King Philip, their teams, and the man following them.

For hours on end Ben thought about Bert. Over and over he wondered where he had gotten to. What he was doing. Whether he was alive or dead. Always in that order: curiosity, interest, dread.

They crossed the Big Sandy Wash and cut south as Ben had anticipated. Keeping the Aquarius Mountains on their left to the east, they stuck to the stage route.

Two days later, late in the afternoon, they passed through Wickenburg, situated north of the Vulture Mountains. Ben rode within sight of their dust, so absorbed in his thoughts. So absorbed he failed to notice that a new actor had come onto the stage. He, himself, was now being followed. By a man attired from hat to heels in black. He sat a hand-carved, sterling-mounted saddle with bullhide-covered tree. His horse was a strikingly handsome, jet-black gelding. He wore neither gun nor cartridge belt. In a scabbard in front of his right leg, however, was a custom-built Zefirelli-Grandee rifle. Boasting a stock and fore-end carved from specially selected Italian walnut. The receiver flats displayed intricately engraved hunting scenes and scroll borders. Its 458-magnum caliber delivered a muzzle energy of better than two and a half tons. It was equipped with a twenty-two-inch non-free-floating, heavyweight barrel. Its twist was one turn in fourteen inches. Its overall length: forty-two and a half inches; its capacity: four cartridges, with the magazine holding three. It weighed eight and a half pounds.

It was mounted with a scope with tapered cross hair, adjustable from two and a half to eight times with a partial turn of the eyepiece.

The three Mexicans had no idea Ben was a mile behind them. Ben had no idea he, too, was being followed. The five players in the drama moved slowly in a southwesterly direction.

Approximately seventy miles distant lay Tranquillity.

• • • •

"This coffee's cold."

"Y'all shoulda' woke up an houah ago; it was just fine."

"When you fixin' to let me outta' this dump?"

"Ah thought y'all'd nevah ask."

Marshal Ira Alsop unlocked the cell door. Out came Bert. He left the remains of his breakfast on its tray on his cot. And handed Alsop his coffee. The marshal wore a square of court plaster on his jaw; it was swollen. Bert started for the door.

"Wheah do y'all think you'h goin'? Y'all still got to go through the dodgers."

"Oh for Chrissakes! Oh hell, what's the diff'rence? Thanks to you he's long gone."

"Don't thank me, y'all could have been out of heah last night. But no, y'all had to go and get frisky on us."

"All right, all right. Look, I'll go through your pictures as a favor, only you got to return the favor. I lost my iron in that ruckus las' night . . ."

"Ah been meaning to ask y'all about that. How come you didn't help us out?"

"Help you out? Are you crazy? I was smack in the middle. Couldn' hear, couldn' see. I covered up like a turtle. My gun slipped outta' my holster; either that or one of 'em listed it. Let met tell you somethin', Allsap."

"Alsop. No need to make it wuss than it is."

"Whatever. A man finds himself in the middle of a shootout that tight, no cover no place, the last thing he thinks 'bout is contributin'. Only creatures on God's green earth that shoot when they're in the middle are skunks an' polecats. Whatta you say, how's about lettin' me have a old Colt? You gotta have one lyin' around someplace . . ."

"I'll do better than that."

"GREAT DAY IN THE MORNIN'!" Bert gawked. "Look out there, it's him! Cutler! All four!" He ran to the barred front window. "Ridin' through town bold as brass. Gimme the gun, I gotta go."

"Hold youh hohses, y'all are not going anyplace till y'all go through those dodgers."

"Come here, look!" Alsop joined him at the window. Bert pointed, waggling his finger excitedly, He was suddenly on fire. "It's him! He's wanted for murder, you saw . . ."

"In New Mexico. That's a good ways out o' ouah tehhitohy. We got 'nough to contend with right heah in ouah own backyahd. Y'all want a gun? Ah'll do you one bettah. Ah'll give you one o' ouah Winchestes and a half-box o' cahtridges y'all tried to sneak out with last night. All ah ask in return . . ."

"Go through the wanteds, I know, you said. Jesus, man, if you're not the stubbornest man in all Creation. Livin' with you must be pure hell for your missus."

"It happens ah'm a widowah."

"Oh."

"Sit down, take a load off. Ah'll go get the dodgers. See if y'all can spot a couple. Even one would help."

He set the taller stack in front of Bert. He pulled away the top one and jumped up at sight of the second.

"That's one, right there. And that one under's another!"

"Oh, foh pity's sakes, whatta' y'all think ah am,

nitwitted? Looky theah, it says plain as day that one's up in Dakota Tehhitohy. And the one undah it, which y'all didn't even bothah to look at, is out of the country. Now, will y'all please go through the damn stack? Please?''

"All right, all right, but if that greasy-haired son of a bitch gets away from me, it'll be on *your* head. An' I'll raise holy hell in high places, just you see if I don'!''

• • • •

It took him fully ten minutes to find two of them. In the second stack. Alsop recognized one of the names. He expressed the optimistic belief that they were still in the area. Bert expressed the belief that Alsop was full of prunes. He left with an old Winchester with a split stock, a broken sight, and the half-box of cartridges Alsop had promised him. Five minutes later he reclaimed his horse. And rode out in pursuit of Cutler, Maria and the others. They were heading out in a straight line. He caught up easily.

He followed them to and through a narrow canyon into a sprawling valley almost completely circled by rising masses of rubble. Stones from the size of his fist to boulders as big as barns littered every hill and mountainside. He cut left entering the valley, heading up a narrow trail, ascending to the top. He dismounted behind cover. Two hundred feet below, he seemed to be waiting for someone. Again and again Maria would go into her bag and produce a pair of binoculars. She studied the road at the distant end of the valley. The only road other than that by which they had entered. It snaked around boulders, zig-zagged upward, and climbed over a saddle.

He thought about taking them. Trying. But rejected the idea almost as soon as it came to him. His curiosity was at its peak now that he had them back. And saw little chance of losing them a second time. He could travel three times as fast as their buckboard. Faster, further, longer.

The shadows spilled over the western rim and down the rugged slopes. Across the valley floor they spread. Lower and lower sank the sun. Positioned almost perfectly over the saddle the west road climbed to. It was still hours from sunset when a cloud of dust arose. Down the west road it trailed. Two riders. They reached the flat and broke into a gallop. And waved as they passed Cutler's party. Dusting on through the valley, vanishing into the canyon at the entrance.

A second cloud rose from the saddle. Three wagons were coming. Bert squinted. It was difficult to see, looking into the sun's glare. But as they descended, he made out what looked like three huge barrels on wheels. Tank wagons. Slowly they came down the steep slope. It took them nearly ten minutes to reach the flat. When they did so, the lead driver began waving vigorously. Maria waved back.

The wagons rolled up to where the buckboard stood. The drivers descended from their seats, excitedly babling in Spanish. From the dusty looks of them, they had come a long distance. Bert's eyes drifted back the way he'd come. Up in the saddle he caught a fleeting glimpse of a lone rider silhouetted against the sun. No sooner did he show than he swung about and dropped from sight.

Below it was old home week. Maria was jabbering as excitedly as the three arrivals. They knelt before in turn and kissed her hand. Bert grunted.

"You'd think she was the Queen o' England . . ."

Two of them who looked like twins began regaling her. Bert assumed they were telling her of their journey. Bert was confused. And becoming more so by the minute. Why had she and Cutler come all this way to meet three water wagons? They *were* water wagons: letters a foot high on their sides proclaimed them to be. Questions crossed his mind like arrows in flight, deepening his confusion. Until a sound snatched his attention.

Shale clattered lightly. A horse was coming up behind him. He turned. He cocked the rifle. A hat and head and shoulders appeared. He aimed.

"Hold it right there . . . Oh, for God's sakes!"

"Put it down. Before it goes off accidentally."

"What are you doin' here?"

"What are you?"

"I asked first."

Ben filled him in in brief on his experiences since they had last seen one another.

"You look a holy mess," said Bert when he was done.

"I've been on the road nine days. I . . ."

He was stopped short by ringing gunfire below. They looked down. And gasped in unison. One after another Maria was calmly, coolly shooting the three drivers. They watched her wave smoke from the muzzle and hand the gun back to Cutler.

"My God,"

"Isn' she somethin'? You ever in all your born days see cooler?"

"Amazing." Ben shook his head in disbelief.

Below Maria had turned Cutler's two men. They set about unloading the luggage from all three wagons. And placed it, along with the satchels containing the doubloons, in the buckboard.

"I wonder how heavy that gold is?"

"Not very," said Ben. "I'd guess about half an ounce per coin. Approximately four thousand. Figure somewhere around sixty to seventy pounds per satchel. Amazing."

"You said that."

"I followed it from Tucson all the way to San Francisco and back here. Better than two thousand miles. Sixty thousand dollars worth of jinx. Wherever it goes men seem to die. Cutler and his friends are just as doomed."

"Like hell, he's mine!"

"Ours."

"I'll kill her if she kills him. I SWEAR I WILL!"

"Quiet down, they'll hear you."

"I will! Look, they're gettin' ready to pull out."

Ben nodded knowingly. "Heading straight for the Burro Mountains or close to. With a thousand carbines and enough ammunition to wipe out the entire white population of New Mexico, maybe Arizona to boot."

"Let's get 'em . . ."

"There's no rush. Take it from me, those rigs move like snails."

"We'll never get a better chance . . ."

"Wait, wait . . ."

Cutler and his men had taken the reins of the three wagons. Maria had mounted the buckboard seat and was preparing to follow them out. She called to Cutler in the lead. He slapped rumps and started off. But the moment the second wagon began rolling, a voice called out, "Mariaaaaaaa!"

Where it came from exactly was hard to determine, other than that it was from high up on the opposite side. It echoed through the valley, ringing metallically.

"Mariaaaaa! *Adios, amada*!"

A shot. Sharp. Echoing. Ringing. Ringing. Ringing. Ringing.

Maris had heard her name. Turned toward the tailgate. She was hit. Back she fell against the horse's rump. She slid off it. She landed in the dust. Ben got out his spyglass.

"Right through the forehead . . ."

"*Vaya con Dios*, Mariaaaaaaaaa . . ."

Cutler and the other drivers had stopped their teams. As one, they rose from their seats to look back. Cutler got down. On the far side a lone rider was descending. He picked his way expertly down the steep slope and reached the flat. Cutler was halfway back to where Maria lay when the man came galloping up. He was dressed entirely in black. He sat a magnificent black gelding. He motioned Butler back with his rifle.

"Bock oop on yourrrr wagon ond get oot. NOO!"

Culter complied. The three wagons started off. The man watched them briefly, then scabbarded his rifle, removed his gloves, and tucked them into his belt. He took off his hat and dried his brow with his sleeve. His hair was snow white.

"Guess who . . ."

"It's him," said Bert, "in the agin' flesh."

"He finally caught up with her."

They watched as Stewart removed the satchel from the

buckboard. He checked their contents. Satisfied, he set them on the ground side by side. Then he picked up Maria's corpse and placed it in the wagon bed. He gathered a few handfuls of grass and stuffed them under the bed and released the horse from the shafts.

He set a match to the crass. Within seconds smoke was pouring upward. Within a minute the bed caught fire. In less than two minutes the entire buckboard was engulfed in flames. A plume as black as his horse wafted upward.

He stepped back. He removed his hat a second time and thrust it under one arm. he folded his hands and lowered his head in brief prayer. Then he transferred the doubloons to his saddlebags, remounted, and rode away to the west, leaving the three Mexicans and Maria where they lay. By the time he reached the foot of the saddle road, the last of the tank wagons was swallowed up by the canyon. Cutler and his men had not stayed to view the grisly proceedings.

"Let's go," said Bert. "Where's your horse?"

"Down the other side. Get yours, I'll meet you down below."

Ben started off. He was out of Bert's sight when the loud rumbling of rocks arose. The sound came floating back to him. Ben yell and cursed.

"What the . . ."

Bert had started away to his left to retrieve his horse. He ran around the rock blocking his sight of Ben. He took one look and wide-eyed. Ben sat in the path. A rock the size of a stallion's barrel had pinned his left leg against an outcropping.

"Help me, help me . . ."

"For Chrissakes, what are you tryin' to do, kill yourself? Of all the clumsy Claudes . . ."

"I slipped. Ooooooo. . . . It loosened. Ow, DAMN!"

"Hurt?"

"It's killing me! It's broken, it's got to be."

Bert seethed and fumed and upbraided him for his carelessness. And shouldered away the offending boulder, watching it tumble down the slope, accompanied by Ben's moaning and groaning.

"Get up," said Bert. "Walk it off."

"IT'S BROKEN! Damn! God in heaven it hurts . . ."

"Don' be sucha' baby. Can'tcha take a little pain?"

Far below, the three wagons came rolling into view, heading directly south.

"There they go." Bert scowled.

"You go after them, I can't make it."

"Go an' leave you here? Don' be a dimwit. The circlin' birds'll be here for Cinderella an' her three ex-pals. When they're done dinin' on them, they'll come up here for dessert. I'll go back to town an' get you a doctor."

"They'll get away."

"They won't. Like you said before, they can't make but a snail's pace. The border's near a hunnerd an' fifty miles from here. There's daylight left, plenty o' time to catch up. Lemme see your leg."

"Don't touch it. Oh, Godddddd. . . ." Ben grimaced. Bert's heart tugged with pity.

"Wish we had some water . . ."

"Get a doctor if you're going to!"

"I'm goin', I'm goin."

He was gone, thundering down the slope as fast as the roan could carry him.

Nineteen

"Allsap!"

"Al*sop*!"

"I need a doctor, quick. My boy's been hurt bad. Got pinned under a boulder. His leg's busted in six places, maybe more. He's out there sufferin' excruciatin' pain, the horrors o' hell. I didn' dare to move him."

"Doc Fothahgill's only doctoh in town."

"Where? Where?"

"Across the street and up the block. You'll see his sign, it's shaped like a stethoscope. D.M. Fothahgill, M.D."

Bert was out the door before the marshal finished untangling the word stethoscope from his tongue. Up the street he sprinted, weaving through the slowly moving pedestrains. He spotted the sign and raced up to the door, pounding on it, calling out. It was locked. The office was empty. He grabbed a passer-by.

"Where's the doc?"

"Huh?"

"YOU HEARD ME! The doctor!"

A woman approaching heard him. She pointed further up the street. "He's up to Dulcie Lanigan's. It's her time, or should ought to be. Fifth building up. See where the sidewalk's caved in? Just this side of it. Second floor." Bert ran off, "Don't say thank you . . ."

"Right!"

He reached the door, flung it wide, and stomped up the stairs. Coming up against another door. In he burst. A horsefaced, wrinkly-bald little man was standing at a table on which reposed his stovepipe hat. He was opening his satchel.

"Doc Fothergill?"

"That's me."

"Come quick, I gotta patient for you." Bert grabbed his arm. The doctor shook it off.

"Wait your turn, friend, I've already got a patient. Down the hall and through that curtain. Mrs. Lanigan is preparing to give birth, Mr. . . ."

"Slaughter."

"Pleased to meet you. Have a chair. I'll be with you in twenty minutes or so."

"TWENTY MINUTES!"

"Sssssh, good grief you are a loud one. Have a little consideration."

"My son's out there with both legs busted, a busted hip. Lyin' in agony, exposed to snakes an' varmits an' such, helpless as a babe. You gotta come now!"

"Will you quit grabbing me? Settle down. What are you deaf? I just told you . . ."

"It's jus' a baby. She don' need you, for Chrissakes. No woman west o' the Mississippi never needs a doctor for a baby. They jus' sneeze an' out it comes."

"Is that a fact?"

"You know it is. Go tell her you got a 'mergency. She'll savvy."

"Are you a doctor, Mr. Slaughter?"

"Hell, no. I'm a workin' man. Hey, hones' an' true,

he's hurtin' bad. Somethin' fierce. It's a matter o' life an' death!"

"I said quiet down." Fothergill's tone was soft but firm. His little gray eyes reflected iron determination. "I'll be with you as soon as I can. I can't leave Mrs. Lanigan. It happens there's a slight complication. It's going to be a breech birth."

"Oh hell, what's that? Nothin'!"

The doctor tilted his head and peered at him over the tops of his spectacles. "You know what a breech birth is?"

"Any idjit knows. Whatta I look like, a simpleton? She can have it breech, reg'lar, upside down anyway she pleases. She still don' need you."

"What is it?"

"What?"

"A breech birth? Tell me."

"It's . . ."

"Well?"

"It's breeches first, that's all. When the baby's borned breeches first out."

"Oh my God."

"That's right, insteada' feet first, breeches first. Hind end. Breeches or britches, that jus' a refined way o' puttin' it."

"Fascinating. Friend, you are a unique speciman; four people in one. Human foghorn, clown, ignoramus, and mine of misinformation."

"Who you callin' clown?"

"Keep your voice down. She could already be in travail." A low moan come from behind the curtain. "Hear that? Show a speck of decency, who don't you? And a breech birth happens to be feet first."

"I know that."

"Why didn't you say so?"

"Jus' testin' you." Bert shouldered past him and started down the hall. "I'll go back an' talk to her. I'll explain, she'll savvy. Hell, you can be back here in an hour."

Fothergill had turned. He caught hold of his arm, stopping him. "What did you say your name was?"

"Slaughter. I'm with Wells Fargo."

"Slaughter. Unusual name. You're not in cattle are you?"

"That s'posed to be humorous? What's so great about Fothergill? Whatja call your father, Father Fothergill?"

"What am I doing?" Fothergill asked himself incredulously. "Standing here discussing names with a perfect stranger! Look, Mr. Slaughter, be a good chap, go downstairs and wait outside. I promise you I'll make it as fast as Dulcie can make it. Although at this point, neither of us has much say in it."

"Oh for Chrissakes . . ."

"Keep your voice down. What'll it be, do you go down and wait or do I have to call Mr. Lanigan out here to throw you out?"

A fist the size of a cantaloupe attached to an arm as big around as a railroad tie pushed the curtain aside. A man five inches taller and a hundred pounds heavier than Bert gaped questioningly. He was roughly as wide as Bert and Ben standing side by side.

"What's all the racket, Doc? Who's this?"

"Mr. Slaughter, Mr. Lanigan. Mr. Slaughter is leaving."

"All right, all right."

Bert waited downstairs. He paced back and forth in front of the street door. Every few seconds he would whip it open and call up the stairs.

"SHAKE IT UP UP THERE, CAN'TCHA? HEY! GIVE HER A HOT WATER BOTTLE OR SOMETHIN'!"

People stared as they passed. But no one seemed in the least interested when he tried to explain his impatience. They simply hurried on their separate ways. After what seemed years he heard feet clomping down the stairs. He jerked open the door. It was Lanigan.

"You still here?" he asked.

"What's goin' on up there?"

"My wife's having a baby."

"You mean she still hasn' yet? What's the holdup? What's the matter with her, isn' she even tryin? What's the matter with Fothergill?"

Lanigan stared briefly. Then rolled his eyes upward as if entreating divine assistance to help him understand. Off he walked. Moments later back he came carrying an armful of towels. When he passed Bert he deliberately avoided eye contact. And hurried up the stairs.

"Tell her get a move on, can'tcha'? Tell him. Tell the kid. MATTER O' LIFE AN' DEATH!"

Fothergill came down ten minutes later.

"It's about time."

"Take it easy. It's a boy, red as a lobster, healthy as a horse. Mother and child doing fine. I can see you're relived to hear it. My buggy's just up the way. Get your horse, I'll follow you."

The doctor took his own sweet time following. They emerged from the canyon into the valley. Bert reined the roan left, preparing to ascent the slope.

"Hold it." Fothergill came up beside him. "What is all this?" He swept a hand over the grisly scene.

"That? Jus' some folks had an accident."

"Accident? It looks like Bull Run. Bless my soul, there's a corpse burned to a crisp in what's left of that buckboard."

"Yeah, she got the worst of it."

"At least the horse survived." He eyed the climb in front of them. "I can't drive up there and I don' ride. I'll have to walk. You go slow, I'll be right behind. I'll try. For your information, Slaughter, I'm seventy. You've got fifteen years on me."

"Thirty!"

The doctor's eyes reflected disbelief in the extreme, but he said nothing further. He was puffing like a grampus when they got to the top. There was no sign of Ben or his horse.

Bert held his hat and scratched his head with the same hand. "What the hell . . ."

"Where's the patient?"

"Flew the coop, the son of a bitch. He's hoodwinked me. I'll bust his neck!"

"I thought you said . . ."

"He was here! I left him lyin' right there, sufferin' to beat the band."

"He made a miraculous recovery, didn't he? Is this some kind of practical joke?"

"That's jus' what it is, on me, not you. I'll kill him. I'll beat him to death!"

"I've got to get back. That'll be one dollar."

"What for?"

"House call. Same thing. Whenever I use my buggy I have to charge." He held out his hand. "One dollar, thank you."

"You didn' do a damn thing!"

Bert fussed and fumed and paid, grudgingly. He stood watching Fothergill descend the slope and go to examine the bodies. The sun slipped two-thirds below the saddle. It would be dark in an hour, he reflected ruefully. He mounted and started down the other side.

Twenty

The wagons arrived at a five-fork road. Marked by a pole supporting five all-but-illegible arrow signs. To Ben's mild surprise, Cutler selected the road at the extreme left, rather than continuing dead south. The choice presented was a break Ben had no way of anticipating. If they did head south, Bert—an hour behind or less—would eventually catch up. Now the chances were one in five he would do so. Ben pictured him arriving there; reining up, cursing roundly.

Ben followed them into darkness. Into the dead of night. Cutler was obviously in a hurry to get where he was going. Ben could not believe it was anywhere but Mexico. Cutler appeared to have a definite crossover location in mind.

Ben was weary. But the cloak of contentment sat comfortably on his shoulder. Things were working out just the way he wanted. At last. Bert was out of it. *He* would be the one to take Cutler. It wasn't which of them most deserved the opportunity. It wasn't which would handle it more efficiently. What it was was that he was less emotionally involved. Less prey to impulse or recklessness.

If the showdown came to a shootout, it would be three against one. he should do all he could to prevent that. He had no personal score to settle with Cutler's companions. No need to kill them to get to him. If that could be avoided.

They did not make camp for the night until past eleven. Cutler selected a rocky spot that resembled the fantastic formations in the Dragoon Mountains to the southeast, great piles of weathered, rounded rocks; to Ben they looked like heaps of elephant and rhinocerous hides, deeply folded and creased. They afforded excellent protection. He hesitated to move in too close for fear of accidentally dislodging a stone and betraying his presence. Very carefully, he crept to within a few yards of their fire; just close enought to enable him to overhear their conversation. It proved something less than edifying.

"How's about lettin' us see our money, Rance?"

"How's about divvyin' it up?" said the other.

"I told you b'fore, I keep tellin' you. It's safer 'round my middle. What if we was to run into some desp'rate bunch an' get ourselves held up an' robbed? If I keep the money in the belt they'll never find it."

"Can't we at least see it?" said the first man. "Jus' seein' it makes me feel so gooood inside."

"It's too much trouble. I got to take off my shirt, undo the belt. Jus' so's you can get a peek? Give me a break."

"How much is there?" asked the other.

"You ast me that fifty times. I keep tellin' you, close to a hunnerd thousan', countin' the securities an' gol' certificates. Twenty-five each for you, fifty for me like we agreed. But chicken feed compared to what we'll get for the arms an' ammo."

Ben nodded. Even before he'd caught up with them he realized that with Maria out of the picture a change in plans would be in order. Cutler had no intention of taking the arms back to the waiting Howling Wolf. Why should he? All he'd get in payment would be a thank you and a knife in the gizzard. But if he went to Mexico he'd find no shortage of interested buyers among the renegade tribes hiding out in the Sierra Madre. He could peddle the carbines one at a time and realize a fortune. Preying on the helpless peons, raiding the little mountain villages and isolated *haciendas*, the Apaches had accumulated fortunes of their own in gold and silver trinkets and coins.

"Rance?"

"What?"

"How come she killed her own men?"

"Whatta ya asking me for, go back an' ask her."

"She's dead, Rance. How come she was killed?"

"How come you ask so many dumb questions? How come you make such god-awful coffee? It's bitter'n wild cherries!"

"Tastes smooth to me, tasty."

"Me, too," said the other.

They passed around a bottle, emptying it; Cutler smashed it against the rocks. They turned in. Ben continued watching, listening. He was tempted to take Cutler while he slept: plant his gun against his face, wake him, walk him away from his sleeping friends. And execute him? He'd never be able to; the awareness, conceding it, annoyed him.

No, he would sleep, awaken early, hopefully before any of them did. He would take him. Take one of the team horses, ride him back to Tucson, better yet, Phoenix—it was closer—turn him over to the law. Bert wouldn't do it that way. He'd finish him here in the rocks. He hoped they wouldn't run into Bert on the way back. Cutler would never see Phoenix if they did.

"I might not myself . . ."

Yes, he would take him first thing in the morning. Disarm the others. Neutralize them. Scatter the horses, except for one. Tie him up and ride him out. Money belt and all.

It occurred to him that he and Cutler had never met. Cutler wouldn't know who he was until he told him. Bert would be incensed when he found out what he'd done.

Eventually he'd tell him. He'd have to. He'd get over it; given ten years or so he might even resume talking to him.

• • • •

Their voices woke him. Bedding down between two large rocks he had slept soundly. But awoke stiff, sore, and famished. He watched them unload the wagons. They carried armfuls of carbines and the ammunition into a cave. Cutler directed the operation. The sun had yet to free itself from the horizon. But both men were sweating furiously. Panting, complaining.

"How come you don' pitch in?"

"Bad back."

"Horseshit."

"It's true. Some mornings I can hardly lift myself outta' my bedroll."

"How come we're stashin' the guns here, Rance?"

"Firs' dumb question o' the day. An' here I was hopin' you'd hold off at least till noon. Why do you think? You think it makes sense to lug this load across the river and into the Sierra Madre? Wouldn't make no sense; wouldn' be businesslike. No sir, we hide 'em here, we go on down, make our deal, an' collect."

"Ain' nobody gonna pay you for guns sight unseed. Not even 'paches."

"We'll take along a dozen or so carbines, a little sample to tease 'em. Don' ask me to explain all the details; jus' watch when we get down there, you might learn somethin'."

They carried every piece into the cave, save a dozen carbines. Working together, they rolled a large rock over the entrance. No sooner had they done so than Ben stepped into the open.

"Get 'em up, boys."

"Who the hell are you?"

"Wells Fargo."

"Is that him Rance? Him what killed Donald?"

"No, shut up!"

"All of you shut up. Drop your belts. DO IT!"

They did not. Instead, all three dove for cover. It was discouragingly convenient. Ben managed to get off three shots, ricochetting off the rock behind which Cutler had ducked. He dove for his own cover as the other two returned fire.

"Three 'gainst one, Wells Fargo," called Cutler. "You're finished 'fore you even start. Toss it out an' stan' up hands up an' you won't be hurt none. Cross my heart."

"Promise?"

"I said cross my heart, didn' I?"

Ben tossed a stone off to the left toward the cave. The single blast of their three guns in unison rang through the rocks.

"Don' go wastin' ammunition, you stupid jackasses!"

"You shot, too, Rance . . ."

"Shut up. Okay, Wells Fargo, las' chance . . ."

Ben spotted a hand with a six-gun. He aimed carefully. It was the top spot of the deuce he had stuck in the crack in the fence rail. The one Bert had blown away so effortlessly. His gun was Bert's. His hand, his eye. He fired. The man roared. And jerked his hand back.

"I'M HIT! I'M HIT! RANCE . . ."

Cutler ignored him. He was on the move. He fled like a shadow to the rock to his right. Ben fired too late. Cutler seemed to be trying to get around behind him. And could do so easily if he let him. The other two opened up; the one he'd hit went to his left hand. He was still caterwauling over his wounded right.

"Kill the son of a bitch! KILL HIM! RANCE!"

Ben backed off. To move well behind the line of Cutler's anticipated approach. But Cutler spotted him and fired. Ben dove back. The slug sang harmlessly off a rock. He was the center of the clock: Cutler was two nearing three. The one whose hand he'd hit was between eleven and twelve. The other: ten. Neither of the two seemed to be considering circling him. But Cutler continued to.

The others had reloaded. They poured useless fire at the boulder Ben crouched behind. Cutler held his fire. Ben could hear him moving between shots. Twice he let fly in his direction. But so dense were the rocks, Cutler no longer showed himself moving from one to the next. Ben placed him at four o'clock and still moving. Any second now he would feel a full chamber pouring into his back. He tensed, expecting it. But Cutler held his fire.

Ben started around his boulder. And drew a barrage. He scuttled back. He had started sweating. His mouth and throat felt as if they were filling with sand. Any second now he would be squarely in the middle. Trapped in a cross fire. He shot a glance right. To reach the nearest decent cover he would have to expose himself for a good five feet. Risky. Very. But his only chance.

The three of them were using six-guns only. The few carbines they had held out were in one of the wagons. Out of reach. He tossed another stone to distract the two in front of him. It didn't work this time. Both fired, hitting his boulder. Chipping it inches above his head.

Again he measured the distance to cover to his right. He crouched. He moved a step toward it. And sprang. Lead sang by his lower legs and feet as he landed. He pulled himself to safety. Close. Too. What, he wondered, would Bert say if he'd seen them turn the tables the way they had. So easily, so fast. Damn Cutler's shrewdness!

It was not an easy life. Not lately. His graduating *summa cum laude*, his Bachelor of Science degree were about as useful at the moment as two extra toes. His high I.Q. had been no help when he had them cold. Only to see them dive to safety. He edged around to the right side of his cover. Hoping it would remove his back from Cutler's line of fire. The one-eyed one had not gotten a single shot off in nearly five minutes. Ben's boulder was roughly L-shaped. He rounded the short side corner and moved forward behind the long side. Peering around the end, he saw the closest outlaw less than 30 feet from him, his gun raised, facing left completely exposed. He fired at his feet. The man started, turned to fire back and took a slug in the heart.

Shaken by the sudden turnabout, his sidekick dropped

his gun, raised his hands, and stepped from behind his rock.

"Don' shoot . . ."

Ben was still down in a crouch. He was about to respond when he heard the sudden thumping of hooves. Up he jumped, just in time to glimpse Cutler galloping away.

On *his* horse!

He fired three times. Bullets bounced harmlessly off the rocks between them. The man with his hand high bent to retrieve his gun. Ben saw him out of the corner of his eye and blew it out of reach.

"Try that again and I'll kill you."

"I won', I swear. Where's Rance goin?"

Ben had run up to him. He fired one shot, his last, smashing the cylinder of the Colt on the ground. One swing knocked the man cold. It took Ben all of three minutes to ready one of the team horses and get after Cutler. It was too long. By the time he got out of the rocks and onto level ground, there was no sign of his dust.

Add yellow to his long list of character flaws, he mused. He sighed, closed his eyes and envisioned a human head on a platter. It was not John the Baptist's. It was his own. A grim-faced Bert held the platter. And ceremoniously handed his head to him.

Twenty-one

Ben sat by himself on the long, bow-backed bench in the hallway. His hat sat beside him. His shoulders slumped dejectedly. He was submerged in gloom. Up the way to the left was James B. Hume's office. Steps approached. Coming from the opposite direction. Ben looked up.

Hume. He appeared woefully haggard. His walk resembled that of a defeated soldier captured and marching off to internment. Recognizing Ben, he managed a weak smile. Ben got up to greet him.

"The three of them are in there waiting," he said, nodding toward Hume's office. the chief nodded. His expression said it was not the most heartening news he'd heard so far that day.

"Mr. Hume . . ."

"Yes?"

"I just want to say one thing. If Bert is fired I'll have to quit."

Hume set a massive, friendly hand on his shoulder. "I'd hate to lose you, Ben. The company'd hate to. But if that's the way you feel, so be it. You do what you have to."

Off he walked. Leaving Ben with additional thoughts on the way from mind to tongue. But not arriving. Lost in silent, surprised reaction. Resolving that a threat uttered and blithely flung back into one's face was downright embarrassing.

• • • •

Lloyd Tevis sat in James B. Hume's capacious chair at his deck. Superintendent John J. Valentine sat off to one side. He was a chesty, medium-sized man in his late fifties. A flinty-eyed, hard-bitten veteran of the company's early wars of competition. Hume took a seat opposite him. Bert stood before Tevis. The atmosphere, the electricity present, the serious expressions on every face suggested that a court-martial was in progress. Bert alternately paced back and forth in front of the desk and stood before Tevis meeting his icy eyes unflinchingly. He had already been asked to explain his actions in the aftermath of the Vollmer-Bolton safe door case.

"Ben killed one of the desperadoes, disarmed the other, an' rode out after the ringleader. He woulda' caught him easy only his horse threw a shoe, buckled its foreleg, an' come up lame. Back he come on foot, buried the one fella, an' fetched the other to Camp Grant, ridin' seventy mile all night through one o' the fiercest hailstorms in the hist'ry o' weather. Got there jus' before sunup, rousted the C.O., Colonel Esterhazy. The colonel dispatched three wagons to the shootout scene, an' they collected nine hunnerd an' ninety-eight carbines an' bettern' a hunnerd cases o' ammunition, preventin' same from fallin' into the hands o' hostiles which Cutler intended to make happen by sellin' to them that roam the Sierra Madre preyin' on innocent settlers. Colonel Esterhazy could not outdo himself in heapin' praise on Ben for his heroic work. Sat down an' wrote a personal letter to Secretary o' War Belknap. Then wrote a secon' letter marked personal an' private to President Grant himself, suggestin' that the U.S. government award the boy a silver medal or maybe even a gol' one for what he did in the name of America, an' for protectin' American people from innocently dyin' at the hands o' hostiles. The colonel informed me of same himself in person which led me to sit down and write letter to both the secretary an' president correctin' one small oversight; namely the fact that Ben is, like myself, a loyal employee of Wells Fargo and Company, the world's greatest an' most famous express company, an' that all Ben did an' I, might I humbly add, brushin' with death no fewer than a half-dozen times myself, was done in the line o' duty to Wells Fargo. An' proudly so, an' that if it hadn' been for the shrewdness an' savvy o' you three gentlemen in hirin' us in the first place, we wouldn'a been able to do what we did in our heroic way. I keep remindin' Ben that the company comes first, which is why I wrote the two letters, followin' up the colonel's letters.

"I also wrote to maybe about twenty o' the biggest newspapers the whole heroic story an' so Wells Fargo stands to get maybe a million dollars worth o' free publicity outta' this for which Ben an' me don' deserve any special thanks or nothin' since, as I say, it's all part o' duty. Still it does give me a special warm feelin' inside to know that by the end o' this week, practically every man, woman, an' child in this great American country will know that Wells Fargo come through again in the protection an' defendin' of that what is entrusted to the keepin' of the company, its employees, office 'quipment, states, an' suchlike. All except Gilhuly over to Fruitland who died at the hands o' the desperadoes in the performance o' his duty which death could not be prevented on accounta' if me or Ben butted in, Cutler woulda' shot Gilhuly then an' there insteada' later on like he did.

"As to the Mimbres . . ."

On and on he babbled with scarce a pause for breath. James B. Hume sat glazed-eyed, enduring the thrashing to his eardrums without murmur or movement. John J. Valentine sat slumped in his chair. His elbow was planted against his stomach, his hand hard against his face, his index and second fingers separated, his eye peering between them at and through the speaker. Lloyd Tevis sat with his face flush with the desk blotter. His hands were clamped over his lowered neck. On and on rambled Bert. So mesmerized by his own eloquence, he failed to notice the stunning effect on his listeners.

Until Tevis loosed one hand from his neck. And pushed it our in front of him. Without raising his eyes, he waved feebly. Dismissing the windy one and his seemingly interminable explanation. Bert failed to notice the gesture.

• • • •

"They said nothing about firing you?"

"Fire me? Me? Son, you got it inside out. You shoulda' been there. I had 'em spellbound. The walls was ringin' with the singin' o' my praises. They put me up on a pedestal. I'm the man o' the hour. Don' be s'prised if they give me a raise. Or a bonus. Maybe a raise an' a bonus . . ."

They were walking down Halleck Street. The sun was bright and comfortably warm. The skies were clear, the air sweet and invigorating. Passers-by smiled pleasantly. All was right with the world.

"You let him get away . . ."

Please, Bert. I thought we'd been all through that. What's done is done . . ."

"On *your* horse. With the money, every cent. You had him in the palm o' your hand. An' let him slip right through your fingers."

"I know, you're disappointed in me."

"No, sir. You're wrong. Disappointment's when you're s'sposed to meet somebody an' they show up forty minutes late. Disappointment's when you go to get the bottle an' find it's empty. No, what you did isn' disappointin', it's sickenin'. Jus' thinkin' about it I start lookin' 'round for a place to lie down. My stomach starts churnin', I start sweatin'; see these tiny beads? An' I feel I got to air my paunch. Sickenin'!"

"Will you stop it?"

"He gets away on your horse with the money . . . Hey, where you goin'? Ben? I'm talkin' to you. Come back here. BEN!"

An elderly couple, the man doddering, his wife securely attached to his arm, were approaching. Bert strode boldly up to them. Then began backing away slowly.

"Did you see that? Walked right away from me when I'm talkin' to him. Is that rude? A man's child's supposed to show good manners toward him. Ain' that so? Be a comfort to him. A beacon o' light in this stormy, heartless world. Source a pride. You got kids?"

The old man did not hear. The woman did. She stared fearfully. She hurried both their steps, forcing Bert to stand aside. He gave way and turned to watch them walk off.

"What a town. The sinkhole by the bay. Folks don't even wanta be frien'ly. Ben. Hey, Ben? Now where the devil did he get to?"

• • • •